He lowered his .45 slightly, his eyes darting from the kid's face to a streamliner passenger train flying toward the Spring Street railroad crossing a quarter of a mile ahead. The kid saw it, too. Behind them, a third car joined the chase. The Merc now topped a hundred.

"The name's Cleary. Jack Cleary."

The kid shot him a quick look, deeply affected, then locked his eyes back onto the road. "Oh, God."

The arms of the railway crossing sign descended, and the warning whistle of the oncoming train nearly drowned out the kid's voice as he called to Cleary

"Mine's Johnny Betts. I was with your brother the night he died."

Two synapses connected somewhere in Cleary's head, and he recalled seeing the Mercury at the cemetery. At that moment, the car exploded through the railway crossing arm and cleared the tracks, momentarily airborne. A breathless split second later the train flashed by behind them, cutting off the patrol cars.

PRIVATE EYE

A novel by
T. N. ROBB
Created by
ANTHONY YERKOVICH

Based on the Universal Television Series
PRIVATE EYE

Adapted from the pilot episode
"Private Eye"
Written by Anthony Yerkovich

IVY BOOKS • NEW YORK

Ivy Books
Published by Ballantine Books

Library of Congress Catalog Card Number: 87-92094

ISBN -0-8041-0269-4

Manufactured in the United States of America

First Edition: February 1988

For
Sandy Dustin

He is a relatively poor man, or he would not be a detective at all. He is a common man, or he could not go among common people. He has a sense of character, or he would not know his job. He will take no man's money dishonestly and no man's insolence without a due and dispassionate revenge. He is a lonely man and his pride is that you will treat him as a proud man or be very sorry you ever saw him. He talks as the man of his age talks— that is, with rude wit, a lively sense of the grotesque, a disgust for sham, and a contempt for pettiness.

But down these mean streets a man must go who is not himself mean, who is neither tarnished nor afraid.

Raymond Chandler

AWOPBOPALOOBOP ALOPBAMBOOM

Little Richard

O N E

The Crescendo Club

Los Angeles—1956

The convertible, a '56 Eldorado Cadillac, black on gleaming black, whispered along Sunset Strip through the hot California night. She had a dual quad, high-compression full bore 365 and racing suspension. Her grille exploded in chrome, and the ornament on her hood was half woman, half rocket. It was poised above a crest comprised of seven ducks, a Gascon escutcheon cradled in a golden V, and two killer Dagmars. She had Sabre wheels, a predatory fin, and was as complex as the thirty-six-year-old man at the wheel, Jack Cleary.

Two days' growth shadowed Cleary's square jaw, which was tipped back at the moment for a meditative pull on a pint of I.W. Harper bourbon. His six feet and 180 pounds filled a rumpled and expensive sharkskin number by Don Loper. He was five days into a bender and felt like hell.

He pulled the Eldorado into the parking lot of the Crescendo, a nightclub on Sunset Boulevard. He knew it would be jammed with several hundred boulevard hipsters, Valley cats and sweet sixteens, misinformed wise guys, and terminally blasé record-biz hustlers. They'd be killing time with seven-sevens and cherry Cokes, hyped on swizzle-stick chatter. But it didn't much matter. Bourbon tasted the same anywhere.

Cleary paused in the doorway a moment, eyes adjusting to the dim light. Center stage, he recognized Guy Fontaine decked out in a black gab monkey suit and flashing two grand worth of orthodonture. He was two-fingering the mike and crooning the saccharine sentiments of "Be My Love."

"What is this, Roth, a Frankie Laine marathon?" a wide-beamed, whiskey-breathed man growled a few feet away from Cleary.

"It's called en-ter-tain-ment, Husky, something you and your hillbilly wouldn't understand," snapped a spunky little bald-headed man who was puffing on a thick cheroot.

"He should've been off twenty minutes ago. How many encores is this gondolier lounge act of yours gonna do?" Husky responded. Then, with an annoyed look, he motioned backstage to a kid with a honky-tonk pompadour and guitar. "Get out there, Eddie."

Cleary scratched his beard, and stepped farther inside. He scanned the crowd, then weaved his way through the blur of bodies toward the bar. He fumbled with his pack of Lucky Strikes, tried to light one with a match from the sodden pack on the bar. A hand suddenly slid into his vision, and a flame flared from a Marine Corps Zippo.

Cleary glanced up at Nick, a tough, good-looking man with the hardened features of an ex-marine, wearing the threads of a high-living man-about-town. The sight of him tugged at deep emotions, uneasy feelings he would have liked to drown forever.

"Where tho hell you been, the beauty parlor?" Nick asked.

Cleary dragged on the Lucky and shrugged.

"I've been trying to get you on the horn for five days, man. Ever since that bogus review board hearing. Jesus, you look like hell."

Cleary accepted the criticism with a tight smile. "I've been thinking about things."

Nick regarded him for a moment. He knew the opposite was true. Then he grinned, clapped him on the shoulder. "Whatta you drinking, bourbon, what?"

"Nothing, right now."

Nick leaned closer, his voice softer now, consoling. "Jack, you knew that hearing was gonna be a kangaroo court job. You knew it was going against you."

Sure, he knew. But it didn't help. Not when he had to sit there and helplessly watch those bastards drag his name through the mud, accusing him of things he not only hadn't done, but had never thought of doing. The kangaroos had kicked him off the LAPD and here he was, so drunk he was sober.

"Forget it," Nick said. "You got it behind you now."

"Yeah." Cleary turned his attention to the stage where a kid with a Gibson hollow body slung over his shoulder was moving in on Fontaine. Cleary pegged the kid as another back-bayou grit-eater three months out of Tupelo with his blue twill Sunday suit, a polka dot colonel tie from E.W. Wrathers, and two-tone oxfords.

"Thank you, thank you, you're wonnerful, wonnerful," Fontaine was cooing in his best bedroom voice.

"Ah, excuse me, Mr. Fontaine," the kid interrupted. He glanced back at his band, a piano player, a bass fiddler, and a drummer, who were moving onstage. "Sorry to barge in and all, but I think you're runnin' a little over."

"The bus station's the other way, Abner." Turning back to the audience, he continued, "You're gonna find this next tunic gem so rightful and delightful."

"Sir, my name's Eddie Burnett, and I do believe it's time for my shot."

"I'll give you a friggin' shot."

Suddenly, Fontaine wheeled around from the mike and let loose a wild roundhouse at Eddie, who deftly ducked the blow with a perfect Gene Vincent 180-degree bob and weave. His outstretched guitar neck inadvertently smacked Fontaine square across the cummerbund, sending him flying off the stage.

Cleary could hardly believe what he was seeing. A

couple of months ago, he might have made a move to restore order. But now he simply gazed in stunned silence with the rest of the civilian crowd.

The kid seemed paralyzed. Time stopped for one crystal moment as if resisting the inevitable future. Then, as if seizing the bull by the horns, the kid cast a quick look back at his band, suddenly slapped the mike stand viciously down onto the stage, catching it with his left foot inches shy of the boards. He kicked it back up and, in one smooth motion, cut a 360-degree spin, dropped to one knee, and snared the mike on the flip side. He screamed into it. The piano, stand up bass, and drums all exploded into the song as a wild shriek erupted from some of the crowd.

Cleary groaned, his senses assaulted by a wall of sound as the kid segued with a groin-screaming split and exploded into verse. Eddie Cochran, Carl Perkins, Presley. Damn hillbillies. Now, here's one more, he thought. This rock'n'roll stuff might last a year. At best. Still, he saw that every bebopper under twenty-five was stampeding toward the dance floor, surrendering unconditionally to its inexorable pull. Strange times all around, he thought.

He looked back at Nick, and grinned. "What you doin' in this joint? You run outa gas on your way to Ciro's?"

Nick laughed and yanked on his tie, loosening it. "Surveillance." He almost shouted the word, but Cleary barely heard him. He nodded his head toward a table near the stage, where a corpulent man all cuff links and teeth yukked it up with two women. He leaned toward Jack. "Adultery case for the wife of that sawed-off hormone in the high-volume suit with the top-heavy redhead. Name's Buddy Williams."

He looked like a hyperkinetic West Coast hustler with a Palm Springs tan, Cleary thought. His wardrobe was strictly Eddie Fisher. He was flashing a good three pounds of ivory and finger popping to the music. "Who is he?"

"Independent record promoter. Has this cozy cabin out in Malibu that I've had wired for the past two weeks. Got fifteen tapes worth of mood music, waves, and size eight loafers hitting the floor."

"Jesus," Cleary replied, dragging from the Lucky.

Nick, in a sightly defensive voice, countered, "How the hell you *think* I cover my overhead: with old war medals?"

"I didn't mean it like that." Knowing Nick, there was probably more to the tapes than he was letting on. Cleary smiled apologetically and loosened Nick's silk tie another notch. The gesture was interrupted by a voice behind them.

"Ticktock, Cleary."

Cleary rolled his eyes and turned. Bunny Von Deek stood there grinning. He was thin, with greased-back hair like a tango instructor's. His after-shave left a sickeningly sweet scent in the air. "Manny kinda thought that mebbe you were here to see him."

Cleary shifted his eyes past him to the loan shark at a nearby table, the real reason for his visit. He stabbed out his Lucky. "Tell Manny to keep his god-damned bra on. The loan's not due for another two days."

"But Manny said—"

Nick's hand suddenly darted toward Bunny's face, palming it, vaporizing his words in midsentence. Nick looked at Cleary. "You lose my number, kiddo, or you just like dealing with social diseases?" He turned his dark, cold eyes on Bunny. "Something I can help you with?"

Bunny shook his head free of Nick's grip. He patted the air with his hands and backed away. "Nope. Nuthin."

Nick pulled a roll of bills from his pocket, and slipped Cleary half. "Few hundred hold you for the week?"

Cleary nodded. He didn't like taking money from Nick, but it was better than dealing with another loan shark. "Just till I find something. This gonna short you at all?"

Nick laughed. It was a quick, full sound. "You kidding? Me? The Joe DiMaggio of private eyes? C'mon, let's have a drink, Jack." He signaled to the bartender. "Hey, Scotty..."

"Thanks, Nick, but—"

Nick cut him off. "What, you rather have the goddamn bottle in a bag?"

"I gotta go. I'll call you."

As Cleary turned to leave, Nick grabbed him affectionately around the neck and Cleary winced, knowing the other man sensed his pain. "Listen, Jack."

Cleary turned, feeling clumsy, awkward, like a kid who was all legs.

"Get a shave, for chrissakes," Nick said.

"Right." Cleary smiled tightly and headed for the door.

* * *

The music pounded at the back of Nick's head as he turned to watch his brother leave. The son of a bitch was hurtin' so bad, you could see it in the way he walked, shoulders hunched over, that goddamn shuffle, moving like he was encased in a steel bubble, or something. *So what's it gonna be, Jack?* he silently asked. *Another week dancing all night with your bourbon?*

Nick was older than Jack by two years, but until he had been booted off the force, Jack had always seemed like the older brother, the one who came out punching.

He started to turn around to order a Cutty on the rocks when he felt someone staring his way. He turned his head slowly, and saw a man seated a few bar stools away looking past him with the blank eyes of a psychopath. He wore expensive threads, a flashy diamond ring, and from the way he sat, Nick knew he was packing lead on his lower back.

When the man noticed his glance, he blinked, and turned his head toward the crowd. Nick watched as his gaze settled on the table in the corner. Was he imagining it, or was the guy up to the same thing he was, watching Buddy Williams?

Nick noted that good ole Williams was toasting his tablemates with what had to be his fifth Singapore Sling. He wondered if the drinks were burying his private pains in the same way that Jack was losing himself in the bourbon. His thoughts were interrupted by the sight of Rollo Augustine, the club's owner, who was squeezing out from behind the bar with a fistful of cash. He was three hundred pounds of Brooklyn guinea-gone-Hollywood in an awning-sized Banlon shirt.

Nick nodded to him, then grimaced and stabbed a thumb toward the stage. "You mad at the world, Rollo, or just behind on your mortgage?" he yelled.

"The kids love this music, Nick. It's like the latest thing." He waved the bartender over. "Foam-rubber dice, Scotty. I want a coupla pair at each end of the bar and maybe a few gross of guitar-shaped swizzle sticks or something."

Nick shook his head. "How 'bout a cut-rate deal on sombreros, Rollo? I hear flamenco music's gonna be big *next* month."

Rollo busted up laughing, then thumb-shuffled his bankroll. "Long live rock and roll."

As if drawn by the flash of the bills, two men sidled up to Rollo. Nick had never seen them before, but immediately pegged them as agents or managers. "All ready, Rollo?" the size extralarge asked, a broad smile on his face.

Rollo gripped his shoulder. "You bet, Mr. Husky." He counted out the bills. "One-twenty for the minimum."

Over his shoulder, the other man, beet-faced and bald, screamed over the music. "Maybe we'll just wing back to Vegas where they understand artists like Guy Fontaine, wha'ya say to that?"

Rollo glanced back at the man who looked about a third his size. "Peppy Roth. Be still my beating heart." He turned back to the other man, and counted out more bills. "And here's three even for tomorrow night, and you be sure he's here on time."

Husky smiled and gazed down at Roth. "Ya know, I thought Fontaine sounded a little gut-shot up there tonight."

"You two-bit Okie son of a bitch," the little bantam rooster spat, and lunged forward as Nick sidled against the bar, allowing the two men to hurtle past and into a nearby table loaded with drinks. He watched, amused, as Rollo and two bouncers restored order. Not your typical night at the Crescendo, he thought, and glanced toward the stage where Eddie Burnett was still raising the decibels.

He shifted his gaze across the room, and noticed that Williams had vanished from his table. He futilely scanned the bobbing, sweating bodies on the dance floor as the wall of sound from the stage seemed to peak. He glanced down the bar, and saw the stool where dead eyes had been sitting was empty, an untouched drink and half-smoked cigarette the only testimony to his former presence.

Nick hurried through the crowd toward the backstage door, his circuits overloaded. Words, sounds, images flashed through his head. Elvis, Eldorados, Monroe, martinis...juke joints and James Dean. DA's and Chevrolets. Lead sleds and feds. Movie stars, mobsters, Ciro's, the Strip. Cars...stars...bars...guitars.

He looked up to see Burnett slide the full width of the stage on his knees to the sound of a vicious back beat, a rat-tat-tat that reminded him of— Suddenly a body, arms outspread, hurtled through the backstage doorway twelve feet into the crowd.

The smoky air erupted in screams. People scrambled from their tables. Glasses shattered on the floor. Lying face up, blood oozing from holes in his chest, his face, was Buddy Williams, deader than an empty bottle of Cutty.

T W O

Bikers

A relentless ninety-degree Santa Ana pushed down through the San Gabriels from the Mohave, and was cranking the city to the kindling point. The heat almost overrode the sultry beat of Gene Vincent's "Be-Bop-A-Lula," which thumped from the Dew Drop Inn, a North Lankershim juke joint, where Cleary had been shooting pool for more hours than he cared to think about.

The liquor and the long hot nights were taking their toll on him. He was bleary-eyed, rumpled, and smelling of alcohol. His unshaven jaw completed that down-on-his-luck look. Yet, he was somehow in tune with his surroundings amid the treacherous assemblage of bikers and hot-rodders, and their eye-shadowed, beehived mamas. He was losing at life, and winning at pool.

One helluva consolation, he thought as he pushed up one of his soiled shirtsleeves, leaned over the pool table, and called a shot. He had run the last table and was lengthening his string. "Four across the side," he called out, a smirk on his face. He shot, and the ball bounced off the cushion, glided across the table, and hit the hole dead center.

He sauntered a couple of steps, eyes shifting from the cue ball to his opponent: a biker who sported three-inch burns, jackboots, and a forty-weight pompadour. Cleary smirked again as the man sullenly chalked his cue, and burned a greasy hole through him.

"Three in the corner." The ball cracked into the pocket. He studied the table a moment as the cue rolled to a stop. "Seven bank in the corner pocket. . . ."

He leaned over and, just as he slid his cue stick forward, a voice called out, "Ten bucks you can't even see the corner pocket."

Distracted, Cleary missed the shot. Without standing, he turned his head and frowned up at Nick. He looked as crisp as a new bill, standing there in the doorway, backlit by neon. Jack straightened up, attempted to throw his shoulders back, then simply shrugged. His spirits were riding a ninety-proof wave, and he covered his embarrassment at his disheveled condition with a cheery grin as the biker stepped up to the table.

"Small world."

Nick looked around at the clientele. "Heard you were in a game up here from a coupla patrol guys I ran into." He shot a sharp glance at Cleary. "At lunch."

Cleary shrugged again. "Been on a streak." He pulled out a wad of bills from his pocket, smiled, and held them out. "Thanks for the loan."

Nick stared at him, making no move to accept the money. Avoiding his eyes, Cleary tucked the money in Nick's suit coat.

"So, is this the bottom yet, Jack? Or you still got a ways to go?"

Cleary patted his shirt pocket, pulled out a pack of Lucky Strikes. "Long drive from the Strip, 'specially in this heat."

Nick shook off Cleary's offer of a cigarette. "Had a good reason."

Cleary fumbled with his matches. One after another refused to light. He shook his head, cursed. "Some jerk spilled his drink on them. Thought they would've dried by now."

Nick handed him a small gift-wrapped jewelry box. "Here, this should help. I'll need it back in a couple of days. To get it engraved."

Cleary glanced from the package to Nick, then opened the box. Inside was a knockout solid gold lighter.

"Happy birthday, Jack."

He couldn't take his eyes off the lighter. Finally he looked up; Nick was grinning. Cleary threw an arm around him. "You son of a bitch." He nodded toward the bar. "C'mon, wha'ya drinking?"

Nick shook his head. "We'll paint the town tomorrow night. Figured maybe dinner at Mocambo and a ringside table at Ciro's for Sinatra's last set."

Cleary smiled. "Sounds good." The thought of the two of them out on the town again gave him something to look forward to beyond tonight. At the moment, it was the only thing in his future that seemed worthwhile.

His thoughts were suddenly interrupted by the sound of a beer bottle crashing and a low curse from the biker, who just missed a shot. He moved back from the table as Nick glanced at his watch and frowned.

"You working tonight, Nick?"

"Every night. Working enough for a partnership of two." He gave Cleary a sidelong glance. "In fact, if anyone was interested..."

It was an offer that came from the heart, and one that had been extended more than once. Cleary nodded, a distracted look on his face, as if he were forgetting something. The biker strutted over, cue stick in hand.

"C'mon, send him a candygram, blue eyes. There's a game in progress here, damn it."

Cleary shot Nick a look that said, *What an ass*, polished off the rest of his drink, and was about to turn back to the game when Nick grabbed him by the arm. His look now was deadly serious. "Jack, you've got to put it behind you. Don't let it eat at you like this."

He nodded solemnly, then smiled, flipped his lighter into the air and caught it. "Thanks again, Nick. Tomorrow night, it is."

As Nick left, Cleary strolled over to the table, studying the layout of the balls. He relieved the biker of his chalk, then slowly and deliberately, he blued his cue tip. All the while, he was stringing his opponent a look the man could chin himself on.

"You should have told me you were in such a god-damn hurry, sport. Twelve ball all the way down."

On impulse, he snared the chalk and marked a spot near the center of the table. Then leaning over, he lined up the ball, and stroked it. The twelve hugged the cushion, and dropped into the corner pocket while the english on the cue sent it banking off three cushions. Finally it rolled to a stop within half a hair of the chalk mark.

In front of him was an easy side pocket shot. There were four balls left, and he had no doubt the game was over. He called off the balls and pockets swiftly and impassively. With the efficiency of a battlefield surgeon, he ran the table in a matter of seconds. He glanced at the biker, smiled. "That fast enough for you? Maybe next time, buddy."

He picked up his winnings from the table, grabbed his coat, and was about to replace his cue in the rack when a greasy, size fifteen paw gripped his right shoulder.

"You actually think you're getting out of here with four hundred bucks of mine?" the biker hissed.

Cleary turned, cue in hand, to face his wide-stanced opponent, who stood between him and the door. He considered the question a moment. The biker was suddenly no different from the jerks who stole his job, and destroyed his life. "A guy can dream, can't he?" Cleary suddenly jerked the butt of the cue straight up between the biker's legs, square into the family jewels. Every ounce of breath exploded from the man's body and he doubled over in a soundless, ashen-faced paroxysm of pain. Cleary took the opportunity to slide, cue in hand, out the door.

Outside, he deftly fixed the cue stick through the handles of the double doors. He looked around, trying to remember where he left his car. In the unpaved parking lot were a good forty tons of bored-out Chevy step-side pickups, full-dress Harleys. But where was the Eldorado? For a moment he imagined the biker's buddies stealing it as he whiled away the hours inside. Anger drummed at his temples. Then he spotted it, over in a dark corner, top down and looking shabby and dull in the dirty neon.

Cleary sprinted across the lot just as he heard crashing sounds against the door, followed by muted curses. The bulls inside were raging. He smiled as he settled into the driver's seat and started the engine. Just as he was about to pull the Eldorado into gear and lay fifty feet of rubber across the dusty lot, the door crashed open. The biker and two lethal-looking gang members decked out in black leather piled out.

Cursing across the distance that separated them, and knowing that Cleary was as good as gone, one of them flung a beer bottle that crashed against the Eldorado's hood. "Next time is right. You son of a bitch!" his opponent yelled.

Cleary fingered the lighter in his pocket. A coward didn't deserve a gold lighter. He stared at the negligible damage for a moment. Then, with the grim amusement of a man plumbing his own personal depths, he stepped out of the car, and slammed the door shut.

"What's wrong with right now? I've got nothing better to do tonight."

The bikers traded incredulous looks as the half-mad Irishman rolled up his sleeves in the middle of a juke joint parking lot, then stepped cautiously away from the Eldorado. The man he had kicked laughed, a hard, ugly sound, and turned to his buddies. "I want this fool all to myself." He met Cleary halfway, then without hesitating unleashed a haymaker. Cleary ducked and the blow only nicked his cheek.

He struck back with a jab to the man's gut, but his fist hit a steel belt buckle with jagged ridges. The biker bellowed with laughter as Cleary stepped back and sucked on his bruised knuckles. Then a jackboot exploded into his side, and a fist crashed down on the back of his neck. He crumpled to his knees, black dots exploding inside his eyes.

Bending his head like a bull in heat, he hurtled himself toward the biker and slammed into the man's solar plexus. The biker let out a gasp as he staggered back into the side of a pickup, striking his head on the outside mirror. He slid to the ground, unconscious. But there were two more coming at him from both sides, two too many for Cleary in his bleary-eyed exhaustion.

A fist sank into his ribs. A boot caught him in the

thigh. Another fist, thicker and harder than a baseball bat, flew into his chest. The bikers pummeled him just as the review board had done, cursed him as his wife had on the day she left. They brought him to his knees. Shoved his face into the dirt. He spit out blood and chips of his teeth and tried to push himself to his feet, but now one of the bastards had him by the throat, and was squeezing.

He brought his arms up hard, breaking the man's hold, but it was too late. They had gotten his money. They were laughing. A boot slammed into his shoulder, and he toppled sideways again into the dirt. He stared up at the neon lights, at the signs with letters missing: E.W. HA–PER'S, BILL––RDS, B–A–K LABEL. This time he couldn't get up and it didn't matter.

Nothing mattered.

Jack Cleary just laid there, closed his eyes, and willed the pain to go away.

T H R E E

The Shooters

Nick leaned against the inside of the phone booth on the quiet corner, waiting for a call. Insects, drawn by the dim light inside, dive-bombed the glass, their collective buzzes like that of a saw. The day's heat had lingered inside the booth and when Nick finally opened the door, the light went out and the warm air rushed in, licking at his face and hands like a hungry dog.

His plans with Jack were shot so he had decided not to waste his evening. Jack was probably better off in bed, anyhow. Maybe a good beating was what he had needed. Hell, he needed something to screw his head back on right. Sure, he had had some tough breaks, but caving in to self-pity and trying to douse the pains day after day with bourbon wasn't the answer. It wasn't like the Jack he knew.

His head jerked as the phone rang in his ear. He closed the door of the booth and snapped the receiver from the hook. "Yeah."

"Okay. Here's how we do it. I want to keep this thing real low key. You hear?"

"How low key?"

"I'm thinking about you, man. The Williams murder had organized crime written all over it. You mess with these guys, and you'll be catching some lead yourself. It'll boomerang right back in your face."

"Okay, I got the picture. When do we do it?"

"I'm sending a car to make the pickup. No uniforms."

"Where?"

"Let's make it in two hours up on the lookout on Mulholland Drive. You know where I mean?"

"Yeah. I know the place. You can't show up yourself?"

"Nick, I've been working my ass off day and night."

"Okay, relax. I'm just asking."

"I wish I could relax. I've got another case I'm working on. I'd love to tell you all about it, but I gotta go, man."

"Right."

Nick dropped the phone back in the cradle, and stood there staring out at the traffic until his thoughts were interrupted by an old man pounding on the door. "Come on, mister. I've got to call my nephew in Fresno before he goes—"

"Just hang on, mac. I've got another call to make myself." He dropped a nickel in the slot and dialed.

The hood ornament on the jet black customized '49 Mercury coupe was a chrome falcon in midflight. Even in the shadowy alley, the Merc was a beauty with its V-D windshield, Frenched headlights with cat's eyes, a dark wicked flank, and a chopped roof-line. From its shark-toothed '55 De Soto grille to its full rear skirts, it was a machine that demanded attention.

Between its '50s Ford blue-dot taillights was a Tennessee license plate and a few feet behind it were a pair of blue suede shoes, which at the moment were duck walking, toe sliding, and heel dragging to the rockabilly beat of Jerry Lee Lewis's "High School Confidential" blasting from the car radio.

Johnny Betts continued practicing his dance maneuvers in the back-alley moonlight as a baby-blue '55 Lincoln Capri pulled quietly up alongside the Merc. Twenty-two years old, with the steamy, dark good looks of a young Presley, he might have been a cross between a teen idol and a knife-wielding greaser. He wore a pair of tight rogue trousers, a blade-thin alligator belt, and a black sleeveless T-shirt. He was a pure product of American street savvy by way of South Memphis.

In no particular hurry, Johnny killed the car radio, grabbed a heavy coat from the front seat, and locked up the Merc before sliding into the passenger seat of the Capri. He exchanged a wry look with the driver, Nick Cleary, who glanced down at the coat in Johnny's lap, instantly hip to the firepower beneath it. "Don't think it's going to be that kind of weather, kid," Nick said as the Capri slipped smoothly out of the alley and up a canyon off Sunset.

Johnny eyed him. "I left a girl back in Glendale in her garter belt 'cause you wanted a sing-along partner?"

Nick grinned. He appreciated the kid's loyalty. He knew he filled a void in the kid's life—as either big brother or father, neither of which he had back home in Memphis. "Got a meet up on Mulholland, strictly public relations with the LAPD. Getting rid of some tapes I'm not too comfortable with."

"The McGuire Sisters perchance?"

Nick shook his head. "Try the late great Buddy Williams."

Though he was impressed, Johnny simply nodded, ready for any eventuality. He tossed his coat in the back, revealing a nasty sawed-off double-barrel twelve gauge. He smiled and settled back to enjoy the ride.

As they climbed out of the valley, en route to the meet, Nick's thoughts turned to his brother. Jack had spent sixteen years on the force, and then one day he had been fingered as the target of a bribery investigation. The blows had come so hard and so fast, Nick had barely realized what had happened until the review board hearing.

One thing he knew: Jack had been set up. Nick

was sure of it. He knew Jack too well to believe he was dirty.

Damn. He should have been here now, teaming with him, instead of... He glanced over at Johnny, who gazed ahead with an expression that vacillated between rapture and nonchalance. He didn't mind helping Johnny out. Hey, the kid was good. But Jack was family, his first priority, and it burned him that he couldn't do something to pull him out of it.

If only there was some lead to follow to prove Jack's innocence. But the case had been seamless. Too seamless. Something would break, if Jack didn't first.

The roadside overlook off Mulholland Drive was dark, except for the bright lights of the feverish city far below; silent, but for the dry, nerve-frayed rustle of the Santa Anas; and deserted with the exception of Nick, who smoked a Chesterfield by the rear of his Lincoln as he gazed down at the valley spread out like a feast below. Johnny was nowhere in sight.

Just as Nick took the last drag from his cigarette and ground it out with his heel, the lights of a vehicle flooded the overlook. A metallic-gray '56 Packard 400 pulled quietly to the shoulder thirty yards behind the Capri. Nick watched as a man in a dark, tailored suit stepped out and approached him, a silhouette against the high beams of his car.

As he stopped a few feet from him, Nick stared into the cold, blank eyes of the man he had seen at the Crescendo on Buddy Williams's two nights ago. *Jesus. The undercover guys are looking more like bad guys than the bad guys.* The two men stared at each other a moment. "You Nick Cleary?"

Nick nodded. "Who're you?"

"Lieutenant Battista."

Never heard of ya. Instead of saying it, he tilted his head toward a soft, distant siren and an angry glow to the west. "Looks like a fire out toward Topanga."

Battista ignored the comment. His blank eyes fastened on the small suitcase at Nick's feet. "You're buying yourself a lotta goodwill with the department, Cleary, turning those over."

Nick scooted the suitcase through the dirt with the toe of his shoe and managed an ironic smile. "Just being a good citizen."

Battista raised the suitcase. "They're all in here?"

"You got it."

"From what I understand is on these tapes, you could've bought a nice piece of change from the other side."

There was something about the way Battista said it that made Nick uneasy. "I could've also bought some lead."

Battista nodded, a smile turning on his lips as he calmly pulled a short-barrel Colt .38 and held it at waist level. "You can get that any place."

Nick glanced from the revolver to Battista's eyes, trying to keep his head. "If it means anything to you, whoever you are, I stashed the originals for safekeeping."

Battista scowled, cocked the trigger, and jerked the gun, ready to fire. "Where?"

"Hey, dipstick!" Johnny's voice leaped from the

dark, startling Battista into a spin. He squinted into the night. Ten yards away, braced against a roadside eucalyptus, the kid was aiming his sawed-off twelve gauge at Battista's face.

"Are you as stupid as you look, or are you going to drop it?"

Battista let his weapon slip from his fingers, then raised his hands. "Easy now," he yelled.

Nick scooped up the .38, just as Battista threw a glance toward his car. Suddenly three shooters rolled out of the Packard, machine guns blazing. Sprays of lead licked the hot night air. The eucalyptus splintered near Johnny's face as he returned the fire, emptying the shotgun. One of the shooters flipped back onto the hood of the Packard, leaving a shoe behind.

Nick leveled the .38 and pumped two rounds toward Battista, who flung the suitcase in front of his face for protection. The slugs tore into the case and knocked him back six feet, but they didn't kill him, didn't even wound the bastard. Nick spun, and dropped to the ground just as another volley of gunfire erupted from the Packard.

"Johnny, come on," he yelled, and raced toward the Capri. He threw open the door, hurtled himself inside, and a moment later, Johnny bolted from his cover and torpedoed headlong through the open window. Bullets pinged off the fender and trunk as Nick peeled away, his foot pressed to the accelerator.

His eyes darted to the rearview mirror. The Packard screeched away from the cliff and bore down on them, its headlights brighter than the sun at noon.

"Son of a bitches are on our ass," Johnny yelled, twisting around.

The Packard was two hundred yards back and gaining.

Hitting fifty on the serpentine mountaintop, Nick leaned over and grabbed a six-inch Army-issue .45 automatic out of the glove compartment and tossed it to Johnny. Nick's eyes locked on the curves as the needle passed sixty. As he hit a straightaway, Johnny opened fire on the Packard.

"Hope you were getting a nice chunk of bread for this," he shouted.

"How about nothing." Nick cranked a turn and the back window suddenly exploded. Glass showered through the back of the Capri.

"Just for fun, right?" Johnny yelled, and rolled into the backseat, firing through the rear window.

Nick negotiated the road like a seasoned pro. The tires shrieked. The Capri hit 80, 83, 85, but it was no match for the 374-advanced V-8 of the Packard, which squealed alongside.

Suddenly the shooter on the right front side of the Packard filled the air with fire and lead, and the Packard crashed hard against the driver's side. Nick reeled the steering wheel back and forth, trying to maintain control.

The Packard struck the side again and again, and each time Nick desperately fought the wheel to keep the Capri on the road. "Better get ready... to ditch it, kid," he yelled.

The Packard slammed into the Capri again. The

road blurred as Nick swung the wheel, realizing too late that they were in an S-turn.

"Now," he yelled.

Johnny glanced once at Nick, then rolled out the back window just as Nick slammed his shoulder against his door. The goddamned thing was jammed from the body damage. He was trapped.

The lights of Encino shimmered impassively through the spider-webbed windshield as the road vanished under his wheels. The Capri was airborne. Nick, still gripping the steering wheel, could hear the soft whisper of air as the car sliced through the heat like a knife through butter. Below, the lights blurred, an incandescent carnival of color—blues and reds and golds, and there, farther out, pearl whites like puffs of clouds. Above it all loomed the velvet blackness of an indifferent sky. He'd blown it good.

His last cogent thought before the Capri's nose began to dip toward the ground was of Jack.

Then the car struck the gully, bounced and exploded, spewing glass and metal and hurling a fireball fifty feet into the September night.

Above the gully, the Packard screeched to a stop. Battista climbed out of the car and paused at the lip of the precipice, watching the flames light up the dark like an exploding moon. "Looks like a fire down the valley," he said to himself with a laugh, then he turned and walked back to the idling Packard. A moment later, it sped down Mulholland Drive, and melted into the night.

F O U R

The News
Hits Home

"... on the weather front, it's going to be a scorcher again today in southern California, with an expected high of ninety-six degrees...."

The words reached Cleary as if from a great distance, then slowly penetrated the fog in his head. *The milkman*, he thought. The milkman always arrived with his radio blaring, like he resented being up before everyone else and wanted to get even. Cleary needed to move, wanted to move, but he was afraid to. He knew his body was going to explode with pain if he so much as lifted his head.

He heard the toilet flush. The sound was like a low

roar that he heard more with his gut than his ears. *My toilet? Who the hell's in my bathroom?* He couldn't remember. His head was stuffed with cotton.... Wait. Something about last night. Aw, hell. Now it was coming back.

He was supposed to go out on the town with Nick last night, but he canceled, told him he was too sore from the beating he had taken the night before from the bikers. Nick had gotten real quiet on the phone. He hadn't lectured him. He hadn't made any cracks about getting himself together. He had just spoken to him as if he were a kid. *Stay home and rest, Jack.*

Rest. Sure. He rested, hadn't he.

He slowly reached his hands up and found his throbbing head. Jesus. Why hadn't he listened to him? He had been too sore to go out with Nick, but not sore enough to keep from swinging by another juke joint.

Now he heard the water running. Cleary lifted up on his elbows, wincing as the throb in his head slid off to one side. His eyes roamed around the room. Jesus. A pigsty. There were clothes draped over chairs, clothes puddled on the floor, a couple of half-empty glasses perched on the bureau, a pair of dirty socks laid out over the lamp shade.

The bathroom door opened, and last night's dreamgirl walked out wearing her red, curve-hugging party dress. But what had been beautiful in the dim light and alcoholic haze now seemed hardened. Ugly. Her eyes were puffy, and she wobbled on her high heels. There was no comparing her to Ellen. No way.

Ellen who walked out on you, jerk. No. Ellen, whom he had driven away.

"Well, sweetheart, what're you looking at? Don't you remember me or somethin'? I can't say you were exactly memorable either."

She rubbed absently at her temple, then slipped on a pair of Monroe shades in lieu of an aspirin, and looked down at him. "Well, I'm leavin', honey. Don't forget to feed your dog. Poor little guy."

Dog? What dog? Oh, God. The pup. More of last night seeped into his head from some 110-proof cavern of his mind.

He heard the screen door slam, and then heard a man's voice. "Is Cleary in there?"

"Sort of."

"Cleary. You awake?"

"Yeah. Coming." It was a familiar voice, but he couldn't place it. He sat up with an effort, and looked around for his pants. Must be in the other room.

He hobbled out of the bedroom, blinking into the merciless morning light. Last night's festivities were strewn everywhere. Empty bourbon bottles, glasses, ashtrays. But no pants. Just then he heard a soft whine coming from the kitchenette.

Crouched down in the corner was Charlie Fontana, his former partner, who was comforting a knee-high black Lab with a white eye patch and a wooden splint fixed to his broken right front leg.

"Ran the little dummy over last night."

Fontana looked up at him standing there in his white boxer shorts. Cleary knew it didn't take more than a glance to see he was bruised, unshaven, and severely hung over.

"We settled on medical expenses, and free room and board."

"Hope the vet didn't think you were the victim."

Cleary ignored the jab as he crossed the kitchenette to the sink where he took a long draw off the water tap. He gazed down on the deserted residential street, then out over the city. He still was getting used to the idea that he was a bachelor, and lived on St. Ives, two blocks above the Strip.

"If it's about my review board hearing, I don't want to hear it." He splashed water on his face. "If it's anything else, it's too goddamn early."

"It's your brother, Jack."

A spark of fear ignited in Cleary's eyes. "What about him?"

"There's been an accident on Mulholland Drive. I think you better come with me."

Five minutes later, they descended the stairs from the second-floor apartment, walked across the lawn to Fontana's '55 Ford sedan. Cleary climbed in, stared ahead in a stupor of shock and disbelief. He barely noticed his dusty Eldorado, parked at a thirty-degree angle to the curb with its top down.

It was just after eight when they reached the S-turn on Mulholland. The roadway was choked by several LAPD black and whites, another Ford sedan like Fontana's, and a drab olive '53 Ford meatwagon from central receiving.

Cleary reached the precipice, and stared down the slope. The heat of the past few days shimmered off the floor of the valley far below as the winches of two tow trucks strained to pull the charred and twisted wreckage of Nick's Lincoln from the canyon.

He spotted two paramedics wheeling a sheet-covered body cart along the shoulder of the road toward their van, and strode over to them. "Wait," he said in a toneless voice, his eyes locked on the form stretched between the paramedics. Fontana followed, a deferential step behind.

Stopping at the cart, Cleary stood there a moment, his pulse skyrocketing. He was about to lift the sheet when a hand touched his arm. "You don't want to do that, Jack."

He hesitated, his gaze still fixed on the sheet. Then he turned to see Dan Dibble, a broad-shouldered, warmhearted Irish American detective in his early forties, and one of Nick's buddies. His shirtsleeves were rolled up and his face knotted with sorrow.

"Believe me, it's him. I already looked."

Cleary lowered his eyes again, wavered another second or two, then slowly picked up the sheet and stared at what was once his brother. He dropped the cloth, turned and donned a pair of sunglasses to hide his emotions as the paramedics moved on to the truck with the body.

Silence quivered in the air as Fontana and Dibble exchanged an awkward, helpless look. Dibble tugged with irritation on his tie, and cleared his throat. "Judging by the skid marks on this last turn, the traffic boys figure he was doing at least sixty when he lost control, Jack."

Cleary gazed out at the horizon. "They find anything?"

Fontana and Dibble turned to a young uniformed cop, who was standing respectfully a few feet away. "Wallet, personal effects." He paused, glancing between the detectives and Cleary. "And a half-empty pint of bourbon in his coat."

Cleary turned to stare at the cop, who, misinterpreting his reaction, hedged slightly. "Not that you'd have to be drinking to go off the roads up here, sir."

Cleary simply held out his hand. "Let's see."

The cop grabbed a personal effects bag off the hood of his car and handed it to Cleary along with a black coat. He fingered the coat. It didn't belong to Nick, but he kept that fact to himself.

He reached into the bag and took out a billfold and a pint bottle of Wild Turkey. Then, replacing everything, he handed it to the cop and turned to Dibble. "Heard you got bumped up to homicide, Dan."

Dibble nodded, then catching Cleary's drift, shrugged. "Motor patrol's handling it as an accident, Jack." He looked down at his feet, then into Cleary's eyes. "I stopped by 'cause, well, it being your brother and all, but..." He looked around, shrugged again. "I haven't seen anything that would make me classify it otherwise."

Cleary glanced around without responding. Another plainclothes detective approached. "Getting way behind here, Dibble," he said impatiently. "Let's go."

Dibble gestured for the man to back off. Angered by the interruption, he took a step toward Cleary. "If I could, I'd rip the godforsaken month of September right out of the calendar."

The sun was relentless, and dust from the tow trucks choked the air. He mopped his sweaty brow. "Been working twenty-hour days ever since these desert winds started kicking up."

He turned, and started to walk off. Then he stopped, looked back. "I'm really sorry, Jack."

Cleary nodded, and watched as Dibble and his partner climbed into their sedan and drove off, followed a moment later by the paramedics' van. Fontana left him alone for a few minutes as Cleary watched the remains of Nick's Lincoln pulled onto the bed of a tow truck.

"Can you get the SID boys up here, Charlie?"

Fontana shuffled his foot awkwardly. "Kinda tough to get 'em for motor patrol cases. It's..." His words broke off as Cleary's eyes suddenly turned on him.

Fontana nodded. "All right. You got it. Photos, measurements, blood-alcohol level, autopsy... whatever it takes."

Cleary drew in a breath, exhaled. "Thanks Charlie."

"Come on, I'll give you a ride home."

He shook his head. "You go on. I'm going to have a look around."

'Jack, it's five miles back to town."

"Don't worry about it."

Fontana stared at him a moment, then sensing Cleary's compulsive need to remain at the scene, nodded and crossed the road to his car. He cast a final glance back, then drove away.

Cleary gazed out at the valley for a while, then sat down on a cliffside rock. He lit a cigarette, his hand shaking from lack of sleep. His eyes lingered on the gold lighter Nick had given him two nights earlier.

You're an ass, Cleary. You did this to your brother. You got in a fight you could have avoided, then turned down Nick's offer of a night out. Look what you did.

"You didn't deserve it, Nick," he muttered aloud. "It should've been me."

F I V E

Farewells

A recent shave only heightened the gaunt appearance of Cleary's face. It was the face of a man who had slept nine hours in the past three days. Bloodshot eyes stared straight ahead as the afternoon cityscape crawled by at a dirgelike pace.

"I was up there till the sun went down yesterday." His voice was toneless, drained of emotion. "It wasn't an accident, Charlie."

Cleary, who was dressed in a dark suit with a black arm band, looked over toward the passenger seat for a reaction, then returned his attention to the back of the long, black '52 Lincoln hearse easing along ahead

37

of the Eldorado. "I found glass, metal shards, a tail-light assembly, and two sets of tire tracks three hundred yards up the road from the scene." He glanced again at Fontana. "And five hundred yards. And seven hundred."

After a silence that lasted nearly a block, Charlie cleared his throat. "Lot of drag racing up on Mulholland, Jack. According to the autopsy—"

"I don't care what the autopsy says." He inhaled deeply, exhaled, controlling his frayed nerves. "The taillight assembly was off a '55 Lincoln Capri, Charlie. Likewise with one set of tread marks."

He locked eyes with Fontana for a moment. "I'm telling you, someone forced Nick off that road, Charlie. And he wasn't alone when it happened."

They reached the cemetery road and, through his rearview mirror, Cleary could see a line of cars strung over a couple of hundred yards. He pulled to a stop as the hearse parked on the side of the road. He killed the engine, but remained behind the wheel, his eyes drifting meditatively over the peaceful cemetery grounds.

On a road just beyond a stretch of grass and tombstones, a young boy, maybe seven, was riding on the handlebars of a bigger boy's bicycle. Cleary's eyes followed them as they coasted downhill through the quiet afternoon, gliding timelessly, like a dream. Thirty years ago, it could have been Jack on the handlebars as Nick pedalled, and death would have been nowhere near their thoughts.

He recalled a bright day like this one when Nick was nine and he was seven. Nick was giving him a buck on his bike to the drugstore, where they were going to spend their quarter allowances on cherry Cokes and candy bars.

He remembered how much he trusted his brother, and how everything seemed the way it was supposed to be in their suburban neighborhood, a new subdivision where everyone lived in look-alike houses and the streets were quiet. It was a place their parents had picked just so the boys would be raised in a safe, clean environment—the American dream.

But that day something changed for Jack. Nick had left his bike outside the drugstore, and when they returned it was gone. The thief had gotten away, and it had been months that seemed like years before the boys' bike had been replaced. It was Jack's first exposure to crime, and it had made an indelible mark on him. He remembered Nick vowing to get the thief, and he said that when he got bigger, they would both get all the thieves who took other kids' bikes.

The boys Cleary had been watching passed a black '49 Mercury coupe parked on a small rise overlooking the gravesite, the driver in shadows behind the wheel. Cleary took notice of the car; its presence seemed somehow related to the pending service.

"Jack, you know what Nick was working on before —before all this?"

Cleary turned to Fontana, realizing he had momentarily forgotten his presence. There was a pensive, withdrawn look on Fontana's face. The expression said he was mulling over something and wasn't sure he cared to talk about it, almost as if the words would make it true.

"What's on your mind, Charlie?"

Fontana peered out toward the gravesite, as if pondering whether his words would compromise the sanctity of the surroundings. "I doubt there's any connection, Jack, but homicide found a body up on Mulholland yesterday, about four miles up the road from where Nick went off." His eyes met Cleary's. "Twelve gauge in the bread basket. Low-level wise guy name of Bobby D'Angelo. Not that Nick would be involved with that crowd personally."

Cleary took a moment to consider the implications, his gaze shifting idly back to the cemetery knoll. The Mercury was nowhere in sight now, and neither were the boys on the bike. A warm breeze had risen and it wafted through the open window, swollen with the smell of fresh-dug earth.

"Look into it for me, Charlie, will you?" He set the parking brake and was about to join the mourners drifting out of their cars when Fontana said, "You know he called me last week, Jack."

Cleary's head whipped around, his eyes bore into Fontana's. "Nick? What about?"

"He was worried about you." Cleary turned to see the back of the hearse being opened, revealing the coffin. "You've always been a fighter, Jack. He was afraid you were giving up."

The words, his brother's concern, sliced into him like a knife. As the casket slid out of the hearse and passed in front of him, he blinked hard. The emptiness in his gut begged to be filled. He gritted his teeth to keep from screaming, and braced his feet against the floor of the car so he wouldn't leap out and race toward the coffin, throw himself across it, and blubber like some kid.

Halfway through the service, he lifted his head and looked around at the mourners. He spotted Dibble and a couple of other guys from the detective bureau. Rollo Augustine, the owner of the Crescendo Club, was here, and so were other acquaintances of Nick's whom he barely knew, and some he didn't recognize at all.

He saw a woman standing back a few feet from the others, a veil obscuring her face. But he would have known that body anywhere, just from the curve of the black dress over her thighs. His hands had traveled every inch of her, reading her like a blind man.

He stared at her shrouded face, and thought he saw her eyes watching him. She wanted him back. *Ellen*. He formed the silent word with his lips. Her head moved, as if she had heard him. But through the veil, he couldn't really tell whether she was looking at him or not.

When the ceremony ended, he accepted condolences from several people around him as he made his way around the gravesite. People he didn't know were speaking to him. He didn't want their pity. He didn't want anyone's pity. He could see in their eyes what they were thinking: *First his job. Then his wife. Then his brother. They say he was dirty, taking bribes.*

Damn them all. He had to talk to Ellen. He hurried through the dispersing crowd to where Ellen had stood. He looked about for her.

He saw her walking away, and ran after her, touched her shoulder. "Thanks for coming. Look, I'm sorry."

"I'm sorry, too," the woman said as she turned. He was momentarily startled. It wasn't Ellen. "I don't think we've met. I'm—"

"Excuse me." He hurried away without another glance at the woman. He was sure he had seen Ellen. God, was he losing his mind? Had he been staring at that woman and believing she was Ellen? At the roadside, he scanned the cars. Ellen didn't drive. Who did she come with, anyhow?

"Jack." He felt Fontana's hand on his shoulder, but he didn't want to look at him.

"She's gone."

He turned, stared at him. "You saw her? I mean Ellen."

He nodded. "She told me to tell you she was sorry, but she couldn't talk." He shrugged as if it didn't matter. "You know how it is with women. Come on, let's go."

Cleary gripped Fontana by the lapels with an urgency that he hadn't intended to show. "How'd she get here? Who'd she come here with, Charlie?"

Fontana looked down at his shoes for a brief moment. "It was an actor, a guy named Tex Harris, plays bit parts in Westerns."

"What's she doing with him?"

"Jack, she's got her own life to live now. She couldn't very well call you up, and act like everything was the same again. You've got to let it go. Move on."

He stared at Fontana, not believing what he was

hearing. Even Charlie was turning on him. "She showed up *here* with another guy? Jesus, Charlie."

His focus blurred. Ellen had been here, but not here. Like a ghost. From someplace deep within, he knew she was as dead to him as Nick, but he wasn't ready to accept it.

"Look, let me drive, will you, Jack?" Fontana placed a hand on his shoulder. "We'll go out for a bite to eat. What do you say?"

Cleary spun around, shook his head. "I forgot. There's something I've got to do. You think you could catch a ride with one of the other guys?"

The Eldorado drifted down the boulevard, top down, the day's heat rising off the pavement into the sweltering night. Behind the wheel, Cleary's eyes were locked to the road ahead, oblivious to the world around him. He barely heard a disc jockey known as the Gator jabbering in a rapid-fire staccato of words over the air as he introduced Lowell Fulson's "Blue Shadows."

Cleary's tie was loosened and his shirt unbuttoned against the choking closeness of the city. His bloodshot eyes were glazed, the wreckage of the past week written all over his face. He had found a bar a few blocks from the cemetery and had claimed a stool for the remainder of the afternoon, which had drifted well into the evening. He drowned his regrets about Nick and Ellen. About everything. Thank God for the bourbon. The painkilling booze was all he needed, he told himself, patting the bottle on the seat next to him.

The Strip floated by him like a bad dream: neon, chrome, billboards, and whores, a garish montage of L.A. consumerism. He coasted to a stop at a red light, his eyes gazing blankly ahead. Sensing someone, he turned to his right to see a hooker moving in toward the passenger door. Her breasts spilled out of her low-cut summer dress as she leaned over and gave him a gaudy, bloodred smear of a smile. Then, just on the verge of a proposition, her practiced lines were forgotten and her smile faded as Cleary gazed right through her.

The light turned green and he continued down the boulevard into the night.

He parked outside the apartment building on St. Ives, and wondered why he lived here, why his past had been wiped away like words on a blackboard. He climbed the dimly lit stairway and lethargically pushed his key into the lock. The apartment was dark, except for the ambient light of the city leaking in through the living room window. He took one step across the threshold, then froze.

The room had been turned upside down. Ripped apart as if a lion had been living here. For a brief moment, Cleary wondered if he had done it himself, and had forgotten. Then he heard a movement from behind the door, and spun around. A man with a hat low over his eyes stood there staring at him from the shadows. He started toward the man when he was struck on the head from behind, and crumpled to the living room floor.

The next thing he was aware of was the sensation

of a rough tongue lapping at his face. Slowly he re-
gained consciousness and sat up. The black Lab
puppy whined and wagged its tail as it hobbled
around him on three legs. Cleary stroked the pup's
head, waiting for the white ball of pain in his head to
slide off to one side. Then he rose to his feet, clicked
on a light, and surveyed the damage.

The furniture was bleeding stuffing, drawers lolled
like frothing tongues, papers littered the floor like
confetti. Turning to the door, he slammed it shut,
locked it. He wandered through the debris for a
while, trying to set things right, but there was so
much. The futility of his efforts drove him into a
chair.

An eternity of silence passed as Cleary stared va-
cantly into space. Finally the detective that was buried, yet still part of him, started asking the inevitable
questions. Who had done it? Why? Was it thieves,
vandals, or someone with a complaint? Hell, he had
made a few enemies over the years. Maybe some badass was out on bail, and heard about his brother's
death. Nothing like getting back at a guy while he's
down.

His fists clenched against the chasm of hopeless-
ness that opened like a black hole in front of him.
Where the hell was he supposed to go from here?
Does it matter? He didn't know. He just didn't know.

He bent over and picked up a framed photograph,
its glass front shattered. He studied the picture of
himself in uniform, arm in arm with Nick in his Marine's uniform, both of them beaming. It was taken
the day of his graduation from the Police Academy.

A long time ago. Sixteen years ago next month to be exact. Even then, when he still had another year of his stint in the Marines, Nick was talking about starting his own detective agency. He wanted the independence, the chance to do things his way.

Nick had been the loner, while Cleary preferred the camaraderie of working with other detectives. And it had worked out well for him until he had been assigned to work on a city government corruption case. He had been investigating several councilmen when he received an anonymous tip that one of them had once been a Communist party member.

He had noted the information, but hadn't done anything with it. Hell, he didn't know if it was true, and even if it was, he couldn't see that it had anything to do with the case. The councilman seemed the only one in the bunch who was halfway clean. As it turned out, it had everything to do with his future.

Several weeks after he had gotten the tip, he was accused of accepting a bribe to keep the Commie crap from becoming public. A thick packet of one-hundred-dollar bills, totaling eight thousand dollars, was found in the trunk of his Eldorado. That had been the beginning of the end.

The councilman resigned in disgrace, and he was suspended. At home, he drank and raved for days, until Ellen had told him to get out. In his drunken frenzy, he had struck her once, twice, three times. The moment he had done it, he knew he had just spelled the end of his marriage.

You've made one damn mess of your life, Cleary.

Cleary looked up from the picture and gazed at the

mirror behind the wet bar. He stared at his reflection, hardly recognizing what he had become—a broken man one step from skid row.

Several moments passed. The man in the mirror, a fuzzy figure, slowly focused. A light smoldered deep in his eyes. His features hardened like bone. Cleary set the photograph on the coffee table. With cool determination, he crossed to the wet bar and, with one powerful swipe, sent every liquor bottle crashing to the floor. The puppy scrambled for cover. Cleary strode over the shards, bits of glass crunching under his shoes like popcorn, and paused at the closet. He threw the door open, and removed a large metal toolbox.

He carried it back across the room and set it on the table. He brought out a twelve-gauge, sawed-off, a two-inch Smith and Wesson .38, a six-inch Army issue .45 automatic, a good twenty pounds of ammunition and, inadvertently, his old LAPD silver detective's shield.

He rubbed the shield against his shirt, then tossed it back into the box. To hell with the shield. The shield was dead.

He set the weapons, one by one, squarely down on the table for cleaning and loading. His hand lingered on each one, a touch like a caress. There was something comforting about the cool metal, the heavy shape, the raw power of each of these weapons, even in repose.

It was time to get a grip, and come out fighting.

❖❖❖❖❖❖❖❖

S I X

The Cleary Agency

The street shone like a new dime, and the early morning sun bathed the city in California technicolor. The impossibly clear sky curved over the city, enclosing it like a dome. The black Eldorado, sporting a new twenty-buck simonize job, stood out among the sky-blue Skylarks, coral-colored Caribbeans, and canary Manhattans.

Seated behind the wheel, Cleary was attired in an immaculate sharkskin suit. His face was clean, shaven, and, for the first time in months, there was a clear, unclouded look in his eye. He slowed at the corner, saw the traffic was minimal, then cranked a smooth U-turn, pulling to the curb in front of a two-story, streamlined, modern office building. He turned off the engine, and glanced up at a sign printed discreetly on a second-story window, which read: CLEARY AGENCY—INVESTIGATIONS.

A minute later, he stepped into the reception area, which was furnished in expensive contemporary design: a comfortable couch, overstuffed chairs. A wall of architectural glass separated the room from the office space. Nick's office was a cut above the quarters of most private detectives, and there was no comparing it to the detective cubbyholes at police headquarters. His brother's taste had always been first-class.

He heard a voice coming from inside, stepped to the door, and slowly opened it until he could hear better. It was a woman talking, and the voice was sexy. "Can't ya see I'm nuts about ya, Frankie! Now put that gun back in your pocket ya big lug and show me a..."

The woman's voice faltered, and Cleary wondered if she had noticed the door. "Can't ya see I'm nuts about ya, Frankie! Now—now—show me your gun ya big— Oh God."

Cleary stepped into the office where a woman stood with her back to him. Her dark hair was piled in a beehive. She wore a tight red striped blouse, a red skirt with a wide shiny red belt, and red heels that looked uncomfortable as hell. She studied the sheet of paper in her hand, and was unaware of his presence. "Good time, stupid. Show me a good time."

She cleared her throat and with forced Hollywood

sensuality began again. "Now put that good time back in your pocket ya big lug and..."

Her voice dissolved into tears, and she tossed the script down on the floor. "Aw, for chrissakes, Dottie. When are you...?"

She stopped as she saw Cleary standing in the doorway, and gasped. "Oh, it's you." She blew her nose with the wad of Kleenex in her hand and quickly composed herself, hiding her embarrassment. "You're Jack Cleary."

"Thanks."

"No, I mean, I saw you at the funeral yesterday, and..." She smiled. "I'm Dottie. Your brother hired me on last month after Verna got herself knocked up... after she became unexpectedly engaged. And seeing as I'm paid up till the end of the week I just thought I'd come in and answer the phones and..."

Her chin started trembling. "I don't know what I'm doing here."

Cleary looked past her to a broken lamp and several overturned file drawers. "You should have seen this place when I opened up this morning. Some creeps must've broken in during the night."

He nodded impassively. At the same time his mind was whirring. "What did they take?"

"Nothing, as far as I can tell. Who knows what they were after."

Nothing was missing from his apartment, either. He would bet a Ben Franklin the two break-ins were related, and the burglars weren't after money or negotiable hardware. He would lay heavy odds that whoever was behind it was also responsible for Nick's death. It was probably too late to dust for prints here, or at the apartment. The first thing he needed to do was find out what the unexpected guests were looking for.

He picked up Dottie's script, handed it to her. He scanned the title page. "'Racket Squad'?"

Dottie nodded, wiped the tears from her eyes again. "TV show over at Paramount that, well, Nick used to make allowances for my acting career, and I've got an audition there at four this afternoon that took me three months to snag. My rent's a month overdue, and..." She grabbed for more Kleenex. "I can't even get through a lousy three lines without going through half a box of Kleenex."

She shook her head, sniffling. "Your brother," she sobbed, "was such a wonderful guy, Mr. Cleary." She blew her nose again. "Aw, hell, I oughta just go back to Cleveland."

Cleary studied her a moment, realizing she wasn't just shedding tears over the fix she was in, but out of a heartfelt anguish over Nick's death. He handed her his handkerchief, and walked over to Nick's office, where the man's penchant for the good life and a stylish front was evident in every square inch of the lavish suite. "You have any job offers after this week?" he called out to Dottie.

She stepped to the doorway, blew her nose. "You mean something a human being can do without having to be hosed down right afterwards? No."

Cleary pulled a C-note from his billfold. What the hell, he could use her help. "In that case, here. You're working for me the rest of the month. I need to look into a few things."

Dottie looked up from the unexpected windfall she now held in her fist. She stared at him, mute with gratitude. "I—I don't know how to thank you, Mr. Cleary."

"You can call me Jack for starters. You can also get me a cup of coffee, black. And you can climb into those files out there and dig up every phone call, appointment, and job my brother took in the past two months."

Dottie looked love-struck. Her eyes were wide with wonder, and her mouth was no longer quivering. "You got it, Jack." She turned and walked out with a determined impetus to her step.

Cleary stood in the middle of the room awhile, trying to recapture his brother in the surroundings. Then, sitting down in Nick's desk chair, he grabbed his desk calendar, swiveled around so his back was to the door, and propped his feet up on the windowsill. Resting the calendar on his lap, he began leafing through the previous weeks.

After a couple of minutes pondering the various notations on the days, his mind slipped back to a recollection of Nick sitting here years ago and marking down a dinner date on his calendar. He had walked in, Ellen on his arm, and told his brother he had just gotten back from Las Vegas, where he and Ellen had traded vows.

"Why the hell didn't you invite me, you big bozo?"

"You know how it is, Nick. We just did it on the

spur. We drove out, got hitched, drunk, and spent the weekend—"

"Jack," Ellen said, lightly slapping his arm, "you don't have to give a blow by blow. I mean a girl likes to have some things just between her and her husband."

He glanced from Ellen to Nick. "Sure, of course. I mean I was just saying we spent the weekend playing married couple."

Nick grinned and laughed. "Seems to me you're not playing anymore, Jack. You *are* married."

"Who says we were playing around before," Ellen said. "What did you tell him anyhow, Jack?"

He held up his hands. "Nothing, nothing."

"Well, since I couldn't be there myself, let me at least take you two out on the town." He leaned over and glanced at the calendar on his desk. "How about the night after next? We'll do it right. All on me."

Jack's recollection was interrupted by the smell of Chanel No. 5 permeating the air. He glanced into the wall mirror and saw a rather remarkable pair of legs.

"I wonder if you could help me?" a woman's voice said.

He slowly swiveled about and gazed at a redhead in a turquoise suit posed in the doorway. Her hair fell in soft waves to her shoulders, hair that seemed infinitely touchable, and she wore dainty white gloves. Her bright red lipstick was nearly the same as the color in her cheeks. She had Ava Gardner eyes and a body that could hold down a U.S. patent.

"I'm Lana Williams." She smiled, acknowledging

Cleary's wandering eye, and at the same time embarrassed by it.

"Any relation to Buddy Williams?"

"Yes. His widow. Nick Cleary was doing some work for me before—before last week."

Cleary rose from the chair, rubbed his jaw. "Yes, he mentioned something about that. I'm Jack Cleary. His brother."

"I see." She pulled a cigarette from a case. "Then I assume you'll be handling his affairs."

Cleary stepped forward, lit her cigarette. The scent of the Chanel was stronger. "That depends." He stared at her, a curious look on his face. "Which ones do you mean?"

Dottie walked into the office with Cleary's coffee, and gave Lana a classic street-chick once-over as she handed Cleary the cup. "Dottie, have you met Mrs. Williams?"

She manufactured a smile that failed to hide her envy of Lana's well-tailored curves. "Just on the telephone. Charmed, I'm sure." She gave a cursory nod. "Can I offer you a cup of coffee, Mrs. Williams?"

"No. Thank you."

An awkward silence ensued, which Dottie used to price Lana's nylons. Cleary frowned at her. Dottie took the hint, threw her head to the side, and walked out.

Cleary closed the door after her. "Care to sit down?" He pointed to a chair.

"No thanks." She puffed anxiously on her cigarette; smoke drifted through her moist lips. "Your brother was handling a personal matter for me."

"Divorce case. Right?"

She nodded, pursed her lips, glanced at the floor, then at Cleary. "Despite everything, I loved my husband, Mr. Cleary. If anything, I was trying to save our marriage." She looked idly about the room a moment, then continued. "Your brother had Buddy under surveillance for several weeks. He'd documented everything very well: names, dates, photographs, and a number of audio tapes regarding several affairs my husband had out at our beachhouse and—"

"You want to take possession of the tapes? Is that it?"

"Yes, I would."

Cleary studied her a moment. "If it's just to satisfy your curiosity, Mrs. Williams, take my advice and—"

"I can't help thinking there must be something in my husband's file that might shed some light on his death."

"I see. If there is, I assure you you'll be the first to hear about it. Right after the homicide boys."

Lana wasn't finished. She walked over to Nick's desk and dabbed out the cigarette in an ashtray. "Your brother mentioned that you were formerly a police investigator."

"Formerly."

She gazed at him, frowned. "I'm not very happy with the progress the authorities have made so far, Mr. Cleary. I could use someone with your expertise to look into it for me. Money's no object."

"Never has been with me, either," he said, and smirked. "But aside from not being licensed for that sort of thing anymore, I've got some business of my own to deal with. Sorry."

Lana lowered her eyes a moment, a move Cleary suspected was supposed to elicit his sympathy. It almost worked. Almost. "Okay," she said, looking up again. "But will you at least think about it?"

"Sure. I'll think about it."

Cleary walked her to the door, opened it. The fragrance of the Chanel became a net that tightened around his temples, his neck. She handed him a slip of paper with her address and phone number. "I'm out at the beachhouse." Their eyes locked a moment. "In case you change your mind."

Cleary watched as Lana crossed to the reception room, her skirt rustling, making a noise like the hot Santa Ana wind, and left. His senses mourned the sudden loss of the Chanel. He felt Dottie's judgmental eyes boring a hole through his cheek, and glanced toward her.

"You're not taking the case?" He expected her to be relieved. She surprised him. Her face bore an expression of proletarian condemnation. "For chrissakes, Jack, she's a widow."

"Yeah," he said, considering the fact. He walked back to Nick's office, and stared at his brother's calendar again. Unable to concentrate, he glanced out the window and saw Lana striding toward a pink-on-white '55 Thunderbird convertible. A turquoise vision, he thought as she slid behind the wheel and the convertible glided down the boulevard. He watched until it was little more than a pink-and-white speck against the light.

"What're you looking for, anyway, Jack?" Dottie asked, dropping a stack of files on Nick's desk.

He shifted his sight from the enigmatic city laid out before him to the files. "I don't know. At least, not yet."

SEVEN

The Williams Case

From where Cleary stood—ninety feet above the craggy coast—he could see a wide sweep of the Pacific, and to the north the pricey curve of Malibu. A small pocket of sand on a shore up the coast was the color of bleached wheat, streaked with two o'clock shadows, and the temperature was pushing toward triple digits. The heat encased him; it was so thick it was like inhaling cotton, and there wasn't even a hint of an ocean breeze.

"In the past year," Fontana was saying, "he must've handled over a hundred different cases: divorce, child custody, shakedowns, blackmail. Let's face it, Jack, it's not hard to make enemies in Nick's line of work. Hell, they were probably taking numbers."

"Tell me something I don't know, Charlie." Cleary's eyes were still fastened on the view. He watched a shrieking gull swoop low through the blue and nose-dive into the water. A moment later, it spiraled upward, a fish wiggling in its beak. Predator, he thought. Predators were everywhere, and unless you kept your eyes cranked open, they were on top of you before you knew what hit you.

He glanced at Fontana, who was removing his sport coat and wiping at his damp face with a handkerchief. "Look, I know how you feel. But they've just started, Jack. Dibble's on it, and he's got the best guys in homicide working with him. Something else'll turn up, man."

Cleary slowly ground out his cigarette on the railing, and gazed out at a lone, becalmed sailboat on the Santa Monica Bay. Fontana, he remembered, had said more or less the same thing to him after he was charged with bribery. *If you say you're innocent, Jack, then I believe you. You watch, something will turn up to prove you were set up.*

He couldn't put into words the frustration he felt right now. The strain of hunting for his brother's killer had left him weary and frustrated. He seemed to be getting nowhere, and the police—the guys he had worked with—weren't doing any better. "How 'bout that corpse they bagged the same day up on Mulholland?"

"D'Angelo?" Fontana shook his head. "Mob housecleaning, far as I can tell. Ballistics made the submachine gun he was found with as the same piece that croaked a guy named Williams on the Strip last week."

At the mention of the name, Cleary turned to face Fontana. "Buddy Williams?" he asked with cool indifference, attempting to hide the sudden surge of adrenaline that charged through him.

Fontana nodded, watching Cleary now as if he sensed something. "You know anything about that?"

"Just what I read in the papers. Local record promoter, wasn't he?"

"Yeah, and facing hard time on a payola charge. Decided to spill his guts to a federal task force looking into mob takeovers in the record biz."

Cleary tried to keep his curiosity nonchalant, but he felt Fontana's eyes on him, and knew his expartner figured Cleary knew more than he was letting on. "Any idea who ordered the hit?"

He shook his head and wiped at his face again. "With Williams and D'Angelo stiff, our investigation's about as cold as the feds'."

Cleary turned back to the Pacific, ruminating on the information. An image of Lana in her turquoise suit, sliding behind the wheel of her pink-on-white Thunderbird, seeped through him like smoke. D'Angelo murdered Williams, then died the same night as Nick, who'd bugged Williams's beach home for Lana. Nick's death, his murder, was suddenly starting to come into focus.

"Stay on top of things for me, Charlie. Anything

turns up on my brother, anything, I want to be the first to know. Can you do that for me?"

Fontana's head bobbed, but he was eyeing the bulge of a shoulder holster under Cleary's sharkskin coat. "The door swings both ways, Jack."

Cleary buttoned his jacket. "Come again?"

"For crying out loud, Cleary, you're talking to the guy who was your partner for six years," Fontana suddenly exploded. His cheeks turned red, his eyes skewed against the light. "I know what you're feeling right now, and I also know what the hell you're capable of. I can't have you tearing this town apart, avenging your brother's death."

The distance between them loomed like the Pacific. Cleary didn't know why it was there or how to bridge it. But it bothered him. This was the man he had trusted with his life, and who'd saved his ass more than once. "Is that what you think I'm doing?"

"Not yet. But you will, man. I can feel it around the next corner."

"Thanks for swinging by, Charlie. I appreciate it."

Fontana stood there a moment longer, then turned and headed to his car, shoulders hunched against the heat, sport coat draped over his shoulder. He was pissed; Cleary couldn't blame him.

He watched Fontana pull out of the parking lot and into traffic, feeling like he had betrayed the man or something. He wasn't sure why he was keeping his suspicions to himself. It wasn't Fontana. No. What it came down to was a severe sense of unease he felt around anyone in the LAPD these days.

Any time now, tomorrow, the day after, maybe next

week, the axe could fall again on him. A grand jury, using the records of the review board, could call for his indictment. Getting fired from his job and ruining his career was one thing. But being thrown into the pen, placed on the same level as the slime he had dedicated his life to fighting, was too much. What was worse for a cop than to be thrown in jail? One thing maybe: being an honest cop, framed on false charges, and locked up with the crooks.

Cleary walked across the lot to a phone booth, dropped a nickel in the slot, and dialed the number to Nick's office. *It's my office now,* he thought as the phone rang. Nick would want it that way. But who was he kidding. If he was indicted and convicted, it wouldn't be anyone's office. Felons weren't private detectives, at least not ones with a license.

"Dottie. It's Cleary. I want you to go through Nick's records, find everything you can on Buddy Williams, and have it ready for me to pick up in fifteen minutes."

"If that's all you're stopping for, boss, you can save yourself the trip. Your brother yanked that entire file the morning after Williams got whacked."

Cleary set the phone back into the cradle. His face clouded as he contemplated his next move.

With the exception of an occasional cab or derelict, the granite canyons of the city were deserted, their dark walls trapping the day's heat like some dire, labyrinthine Dutch oven. The light at Grand and Seventy turned green. Seconds later Cleary tromped on

the Eldorado's gas pedal and blew through the inter-
section, top up, headed north.

He cruised through the warm night air along
Grand, keeping to the legal speed limit. He passed
Temple Avenue, pulled the Caddy back to trolling
speed, then glanced out the driver's window at the
federal building on the corner. Seven stories of dark
and impassive concrete and stone stared back at him.

He parked along Grand Street, then crossed the
street and walked half a block to an alley behind the
building. Without a second thought, he lugged a gar-
bage can over to one of the steel-reinforced windows,
climbed on top of it, and opened a ten-inch jimmy
blade. He slipped it through the midsill and began
working on the latch. Within a couple of minutes, the
window slid slowly open.

Armed with a four-cell flashlight and burglar's
tools, Cleary crawled through the window with the
efficiency of a B&E artist. He took a moment to get
his bearings in the darkened building, then closing
the window, he moved down the hallway, playing his
light along the wall.

Ten feet short of the main corridor, he stopped. His
light was shining on another window facing the alley.
It was ajar a couple of inches. *Woulda saved myself
lots of trouble if I'd known they'd kept one open for
me*, he thought with irritation. His heart sped up as
he reached the main corridor and paused. No guard
in sight. Then he headed down the dimly lit hall toward a stairwell. *If you're caught, pal, it's indictment
time for sure.*

He opened the door to the staircase. The silence

was thicker than oil, except for the loud drum of his heart. Sweat had leaped across his back, oozed down the sides of his face. He was about to ascend the stairs when he heard a door shut, then footsteps on the stairs. Someone was coming down. He took a step back toward the corridor, and was wondering which way to turn, when suddenly the shriek of a security alarm sliced through the silence.

Damn it. What the hell? He froze, wondering how he could've been detected. He had a momentary vision of himself being hauled off by the feds, shoved in a cell, the key thrown away. *Move, man.*

The approaching sound of footsteps on the stairs overhead galvanized him. He leaped back into the corridor, and bolted down the side hallway. He glanced back, spotted the shadow of another figure narrowing the distance between them. He dashed to the window he had entered by and hurled himself through it.

He hung a moment from the sill, then dropped some ten feet into the alley. The sound of his breathing filled the air. His heart hammered. He sprinted off in the direction of Grand Street, but was stopped cold by the sight of a patrol car. Its lights out, its radio crackling, it pulled to a strategic halt near the mouth of the alley.

Aw, shit, You sure do pick 'em, Cleary. No ordinary B&E for you, but a federal building for a federal rap.

Cleary pressed against the wall. *Do not panic.* He looked to his left in the opposite direction for a possible escape route. Hulking in the shadows, at one with the night, was a '49 Mercury. He estimated it was ten long strides away. After a glance over his shoulder to the patrol car, he ducked low and scampered toward the vehicle.

Pressing himself against the wall again, he saw the car was empty. He was considering the idea of rolling underneath it to hide from the police when suddenly a pair of legs were hanging from a window, probably the one that had been partially open.

A moment later, a body dropped into a pile of rubbish. "Man, oh, man," the kid hissed, as he leaped up and spotted the patrol car. He scampered to the Mercury. Cleary timed his approach, ripping open the passenger door just as the kid slid behind the wheel. It was a punk with a pompadour, his T-shirt sleeve rolled up to his shoulder over a pack of cigarettes, guilt and fear written all over his mug. "What the hell!" His jaw slackened at the sight of Cleary pointing a .45 automatic square at his face. "Who are you?"

The sound of sirens pounded in Cleary's ears. He glanced up the alley where two patrol cars now blocked the end. "A guy with a gun. Now get this eyesore moving."

The kid switched on the ignition. "Like I was gonna stick around for autographs."

He suddenly popped the clutch and nearly threw Cleary into the windshield as the Merc rocketed in reverse down the alley. Smoke poured off the burning rear rubber, but the lead patrol car was only twenty yards off the front end and gaining, barreling toward them like some creature out of hell.

They were going at least thirty miles an hour—

backwards—when Cleary glanced out the windshield. The patrol car was within five feet, its high beams burning into his eyes, nearly blinding him. Its gumball was flashing, its siren wailing.

"Weird perspective," the kid shouted, clutching his suicide knob.

Suddenly he cranked his steering wheel clockwise a full three revolutions as the Mercury exploded out the west end of the alley onto Broadway. The maneuver sent the roadster into a perfect one-eighty whipslide spin that made Cleary so dizzy he could have puked.

The kid double-clutched into second without missing a beat and buzzed into the alley across Broadway. Pedal to the metal, he glanced into the rearview mirror at the pursuing patrol cars, now eighty yards off his rear. He looked quickly at Cleary as he shifted into third. "Okay, big shot, now you mind telling me—"

He bit the words in half as Cleary shoved the .45 hard into his ribs. "Shut up and drive, sucker. Just keep on moving, got that?"

The kid blasted out of the alley at fifty plus, then cranked the wheel hard left into a four-wheel, tire-screaming drift up Spring Street. Cleary tensely divided his attention between the road ahead, and the cops behind. "Who are you? What were you doing back there?" he screamed at the kid, who glanced down at the gun in his side.

"Betty Crocker. I was baking a friggin' cake." He cast a quick glance up at the screaming gumballs in his mirror, then slam-shifted into fourth as Cleary raised the .45 to his right cheek and pulled back the hammer.

"You may have the shooter, pal, but I got the wheel. And this 'eyesore' is doing seventy."

Cleary, without a word, shifted the barrel two inches to the right and pulled the trigger. The .45 discharged directly in front of the kid's face, shattering his driver's side window. "Ask me if I care."

The kid slammed a hand over his ear. "Jeez, what are you doing, man? You nuts?"

"You want to see if I can get any closer?" He cocked the gun again.

"All right. All right." He held up a hand. The speedometer needle hit eighty as they raced down Sunset. "I was rifling through some FBI files."

"What for?"

"For info on a guy by the name of Buddy Williams. A dead guy."

Just as that little tidbit registered with Cleary, the kid's eyes widened with panic. "Holy sh—"

He cranked the wheel hard right, missing a tractor trailer by a few feet. Then he swerved into a quick left up North Spring, the cops, matching every maneuver, still burning rubber on his tail.

"Keep talking," Cleary shouted.

"Someone had cleaned it out already. Now who the hell are you, man?"

He lowered his .45 slightly, his eyes darting from the kid's face to a streamliner passenger train flying toward the Spring Street railroad crossing a quarter of a mile ahead. The kid saw it, too. Behind them, a third car joined the chase. The Merc now topped a hundred.

"The name's Cleary. Jack Cleary."

The kid shot him a quick look, deeply affected, then locked his eyes back onto the road. "Oh, God."

The arms of the railway crossing sign descended, and the warning whistle of the oncoming train nearly drowned out the kid's voice as he called out to Cleary.

"Mine's Johnny Betts. I was with your brother the night he died."

Two synapses connected somewhere in Cleary's head, and he recalled seeing the Mercury at the cemetery. At that moment, the car exploded through the railway crossing arm and cleared the tracks, momentarily airborne. A breathless split second later the train flashed by behind them, cutting off the patrol cars.

E I G H T

Recovery

TINY NAYLOR'S was the neon name across the front of the atomic-age drive-in coffee shop. Its delta wings were spread like a B-29 poised for takeoff from the corner of Sunset and La Brea. Inside the stainless-steel-and-Formica "fuselage," Cleary and Johnny Betts were deep in conversation in a corner booth.

"You didn't get any names, plate numbers, anything at all?" Cleary asked. He sipped at his coffee, then gave an annoyed look at the miniature jukebox selector on the wall of their booth as Elvis sang "Poor Boy."

Betts looked up from his plate of burgers and fries,

stabbed his straw at the bottom of his glass of Coke. "I would've asked for a business card, but I was too busy combing lead outta my hair."

Cleary, who'd noticed his bandaged arm, nodded. Then he slid out of the booth. "Gonna call a cab." He walked over to the phone in the corner, slipped in his nickel, and dialed all fives, the number one of the cab company's cars wore on their sides. The number was busy. He hung up, glanced over to where Betts was weaving his shoulders to the tune and diving into his food as if he hadn't eaten all day.

He would have preferred Betts being one of his brother's killers, instead of a sidekick. But he believed him. It was just like Nick to give some hard-luck kid, even a hipster-hot-rodder, a break. Yeah, Nick, the softie. Nick the savior. Nick. He probably had him doing some of the tedious footwork, and on his final night had called him in as a backup.

Nick had never said a word about Betts, but that wasn't unusual. He'd always acted as if his business dealings were military secrets. Now his death seemed just as classified. Stamped TOP SECRET. Not even the guy who was with him at the end knew much about it.

So far, all he had found out from Betts was what he already suspected: that the tapes were what his killers were after, and that Nick thought he was handing them over to the law. But if they had gotten the tapes, why the break-ins?

He dialed the number again, and this time it started ringing. The dispatcher's voice repeated the name of the company and he ordered a cab to Tiny Naylor's.

"Give him five or ten minutes."

Cleary hung up, and returned to the table where Betts frowned up at him. "Why you figure they wanted those surveillance tapes so bad?"

"Must've been something on 'em that tied them to the Williams hit. The mob likes to sweep up its tracks, keep everything nice and neat and clean. No complications. You sure that was all they were after?"

"Far as I know. I couldn't hear what they were talking about, but suddenly Mr. Slick in the fancy duds pulled his gun on Nick, and everything went berserk." He jammed the last of his first burger in his mouth, chewed, swallowed. "You got any reason to believe they were after something else?"

Cleary just shrugged. Johnny plugged a nickel into the boothside juke and punched a couple of tunes. Then, an inner burden showing on his face, he looked over at Cleary, his brow knitting in a frown.

"Your brother was the kind of cat I'd follow into a burning house with a can of high octane under each arm." He made a fist; struck the table in frustration. "I bailed outta his wheels, Cleary, believing he was halfway out the door already."

"You think I'd be sittin' here if I thought you were responsible for his death?"

Betts shrugged. "I'm just telling you what happened. That's all."

You want me to absolve you, kid? Okay, you're forgiven. He nodded. "You said you'd been working for Nick. For how long?"

"Off and on, ever since I hit town. 'Bout a year now, I guess."

"You were his public relations man, no doubt." Cleary gazed impassively at Betts, just a hint of a smile curling on his lips as the last few bars of "Poor Boy" wound down. He glanced out the floor-to-ceiling plate-glass window to the parking lot, looking for the cab.

Betts stuffed a handful of fries into his mouth, and washed it down with a monstrous Coke, acting as if he hadn't heard Cleary. Then he tossed his head with a look that said, "Nice try wise guy."

"He had me doin' surveillance, tail jobs, back-up gigs like—like that night." He looked down a moment, a thought taking form. "Which reminds me..."

He broke off in midstream as the boothside juke segued into Dinah Shore's "Lavender Blue," a saccharine piece of pop horror guaranteed to turn the stomach of any red-blooded rock and roller. He stared at the jukebox. "What the hell. Now I didn't—"

He slammed the box with his fist, then turned to the white-uniformed waitress passing by in her tractor-tread orthopaedics. "Hey, I punched my last nickel in on 'Susie Q,' and 'Race with the Devil,' and this sumbitch's playing Dinah Shore, for chrissake."

The waitress tilted her four-story bouffant and smiled at Cleary. "Thank God for small favors."

She passed on, leaving a visibly disturbed Betts cringing as the song continued dripping out of the errant juke. Then, burying his second burger beneath a mound of catsup, relish, onions, and pickles, he made a futile attempt to regain his prior train of thought.

"Like I was saying, if you plan on going after these guys you're gonna need..."

His eyes slid over to the juke as Dinah Shore sang: "If your dilly dilly heart feels a dilly dilly way, and if you answer 'yes'..."

He smacked the box again. "Damn, I hate that song." Looking back to Cleary, he continued, "... someone with the proper expertise and savvy who can—for crying out loud, man. I mean—"

He pushed the reject button again and again to no avail as Dinah sang on: "... on a dilly dilly day I'll be wed in a dilly dilly dress, ah, lavender blue, dilly, dilly..."

"... who can work the streets without..." Distracted again, he clenched his fist. "... attracting a lot of attention."

"If you were king, dilly dilly I'd be the queen, and a dilly dilly..."

Crazed by Dinah's relentless warbling, Betts wheeled about, cracked his fist down on the top of the box, ripping the entire unit off its wall mount. The music was finally silenced, and every head in the restaurant was turned toward them.

Stunned, Betts stared at his handiwork for a moment, then, glancing guardedly at Cleary, he attempted lamely to cover up the evidence with a couple of dirty napkins and plates.

"You mean someone like yourself? Is that the idea?" Cleary asked.

"Yeah. More or less."

Cleary looked out the window and saw the taxi pulling into the parking lot. He slid out of the booth, took a good look at the tattooed rockabilly rebel, who stared defiantly back at him over the remains of the meal and the mutilated jukebox. "I'll see you around, Johnny."

Betts erupted out of the booth, almost knocking the table over, and grabbed Cleary's arm. "Listen, your brother didn't hire me just for my social connections, Cleary. I can handle anything from .38s to full automatics, break and enter with the best of 'em, and hot-wire a car in under twenty seconds."

"College man, huh?"

"I'm as hot to nail these sons of bitches as you are, man."

Cleary looked at him another moment. "Stay out of it, kid. For your good, and mine." He dropped a couple of dollars on the table to cover the cost of Betts's meal, turned and headed out the door to the waiting taxi.

The taxi cruised down Sunset, headed to Grand. Another hour and the city would be awakening to the dawn. But now, in the early morning lull, the city looked uninhabited, like a scene from that movie a couple years back, *The Day the Earth Stood Still.*

Cleary thought about an old cliche about criminals: They always return to the scene of the crime. There'd been a lot of times he had wished that was really true, but now, ironically, that was just what he was doing. Returning to pick up his car.

He had a feeling it would be wise to be prepared

with an alibi in case anyone looking into the break-in got curious about the Eldorado across the street from the federal building. He asked the driver, a beefy New York transplant sporting a Brooklyn Dodgers cap, to pull into a gas station.

He placed a deposit on a five-gallon can and filled it with high-octane ethanol. His story was he had run out of gas earlier, and wound up in a bar until he had gotten around to retrieving the Eldorado.

As they pulled out of the gas station, Cleary leaned forward and asked the driver if there was anyplace nearby where he could pick up a bottle. "At this hour?" the driver asked, glancing back. "You should have thought of that a few hours ago."

After a moment, the driver looked at him through his rearview mirror, then reached under the seat "If you want a short one, I can handle that for you, pal."

He held up a paper bag with the top of a pint bottle sticking out the top. "There's only a couple swallows left, and I'd just as soon get rid of it."

Cleary smiled at his luck. "That's all I need," he said, reaching for the bottle. "You're a long way from home for a Dodger fan. Think they'll beat the Yankees in the Series?" he asked, taking a slug of the whiskey.

"As long as Newcombe's in there, I say they'll take it in five games. If Newcombe gets hurt, it'll take seven."

"Might be their turn to lose this year."

"If that happens, the bums oughta get their butts kicked out of the park."

As the driver talked on about the upcoming Series,

Cleary poured the last of the booze into his palm and slapped it on himself like after-shave.

The taxi turned on Grand, and they were within a block of the federal building when Cleary saw just what he'd suspected. A break-in of a federal facility had warranted more than a brief B&E report. Three patrol cars were in sight, two across the street near the alley, and another half a block down from his own. Besides that, he saw a couple of unmarked cars, probably feds. He gazed at the Eldorado, black, sleek, a lone whale beached on concrete, and suspicious as hell. Swell. He needed this.

The boys probably didn't have much yet, besides the description of the jazzed-up Mercury. Getting out of the taxi and climbing into the Caddy at this hour was going to attract attention. No doubt about it. The taxi slowed.

"This where you want, mister?"

Cleary wavered now that he was here. "Listen, buddy, I don't care to talk to these cops. Got a stack of unpaid tickets in a drawer back at home. These guys will lock me up and throw away the key."

"You'll get another one if you don't move that car by eight." When Cleary didn't answer, he shrugged. "So, where you want me to take you and the gas can?"

He was about to give him his St. Ives address when he spotted a familiar face on the street. Dan Dibble was standing under a streetlight talking with a couple of patrolmen.

"So where do we go, mister?"

"Around the corner."

"'Around the corner,'" he repeated, as if he thought Cleary had a few loose screws.

"Right. Some problem with that?"

"Nope. You're paying." He shrugged. "Suit yourself, pal."

He paid the driver, thanked him for the drink, and stepped out with the gas can. He knew he would have to pass Dibble and the others to get to the Eldorado, and that was exactly what he wanted. Dibble knew the Eldorado, and there was no way he would have passed it without noticing it.

Cleary would confront him right here and now.

The big Irishman spotted him from half a block away. "You up early, Cleary? Or is it out late?"

"You got it." The patrolmen and Dibble scrutinized him. "What's going on here?" he asked, slurring his voice.

"We had a couple of unexpected late-night visitors at the federal building a couple of hours ago. And what might you be doing in the neighborhood?"

Cleary placed the gas can on the sidewalk, took out a pack of Lucky Strikes, and tapped one out. "Ran out of gas earlier crossing town, then got hung up at Junior's." The nightclub was less than a mile away and always packed, so it would be hard to prove he wasn't there.

Dibble's eyes widened as Cleary, wobbling slightly, pulled out his lighter. "Hey, Jack, hold it. Lemme move the can for chrissake."

"Oh. Yeah. Jesus, I'm getting forgetful."

Dibble pushed the can away with his foot, and

Cleary flicked his lighter a couple of times. "You sure you can drive home?"

"Well, I am a little loose, but I don't want my car towed."

"Tell you what. I'll drive you back, and have a patrol car pick me up."

Cleary didn't like the idea, but he didn't have much choice. He played a good drunk, all right. Too good. The ironies of the evening were piling up like kids at a Presley concert.

They walked over to the car. Cleary picked up the gas can, but a visibly nervous Dibble said, "Look, you sit down and let me pour the gas."

Cleary gave a drunken salute and plopped down on the curb. Suddenly he was worried about the gas. He couldn't remember when he had filled up last. Suppose the stuff just overflowed? He could see it now: Dibble suspicious, Cleary stammering through some half-assed excuse, the feds strolling over....

But a few moments later, Dibble was behind the wheel, en route to Cleary's. "I'm ready to call it a night. Started at nine this morning," Dibble said, stifling a yawn.

"What you doing at a B&E?" Cleary said, hanging his head at a properly soused tilt.

"I was on my way home when I was called into a chase. Some geared-up greaser in a hopped-up '49 Merc. Never got close to him myself."

"What was taken, you know?"

"Maybe files. They'll be checking in the morning. Could be an inside job of some sort, or maybe somebody was cleaning house on some incriminating evidence."

Incriminating: Hey yeah, Dibble, you got that right.

Cleary noticed him glance down at the gauge and his heart skipped a beat. "Say, Jack, according to this, you've got three-quarters of a tank of gas."

Damn. "Hit it with your hand. That needle keeps sticking."

Dibble brought his fist down hard against the glass. Too hard, like he was maybe imagining it was someone's head. "Nope. It's stuck."

"That damn gauge has been stuck on three-quarters for a week. That's part of the problem. I'm never sure when I'm gonna run out."

Dibble frowned at him, quiet a moment. "If I were you, I'd get that fixed real fast. Never know where you might run out next time."

N I N E

At the Beach

Standing back from the shore under the shade of a palm tree, Cleary gazed out at the Channel Islands, visible far to the north against the lapis sky. It was hot and so still, he could hear the waves as they broke against the sand. The light made everything glisten and deepened the colors, almost as if the sea, the beach, and sky were covered with a light coat of varnish.

He shifted his gaze to the figure of a woman running through the sun-dappled ebb tide along Trancas Beach. She seemed illusory as she moved through the shimmering waves of heat that rose off the sand.

Then, as she drew closer and slowed to a walk, Cleary recognized her.

Poured into a one-piece black swimsuit, her damp auburn hair trembling over a glistening tan, Lana Williams was the loveliest sight he had seen in he didn't know how long.

Cleary, his eyes shaded by sunglasses, nodded as she approached. "Hi, hope I'm not interrupting anything important."

She smiled and caught her hair at the back of her neck with her hand. "Well, Mr. Cleary. I didn't expect to see you again. What brings you out to the beach?"

"It's ninety-eight degrees in town." Her face burned through to the back of his brain.

"It's not much better out here. Come on up."

She trotted up the short flight of stairs to the deck, offering Cleary a view of her from the back—the long curve of her spine, terrific legs, an incredible ass. She whisked a fresh towel from a chair and began patting herself dry. She caught his eye, smiled. "Any other news from town, Mr. Cleary? Other than the weather."

Cleary leaned against the railing, hands in his pockets. "If you mean your husband's file, the answer's no. I haven't been able to track it down yet."

Lana accepted this bit of news with apparent equanimity. Then, slipping into a short beach robe, she began brushing her hair. Cleary watched a swell gathering momentum, rising, then crashing as it rolled toward shore.

"Mr. Cleary, you don't seem like the kind of man

who would drive all this way just to look at the waves."

"You're right." He took off his sunglasses. "That job offer. Is it still open?"

Lana ran the brush through her hair one more time, then patted it against her palm as she looked at him. "You bet. Have you had lunch yet?"

Cleary shook his head.

"Well, you're invited." She turned to a maid setting a table on the deck. *"Habran dos personas para la comida, Teresa."*

She looked pensively at Cleary. "What changed your mind about looking into Buddy's murder?"

"Let's just say I've developed a personal interest in the matter," he said, slipping his sunglasses back on.

The answer was intentionally vague, but she didn't seem to notice. Or if she did, she decided not to press for clarification. They walked over to the table and sat down. Lana slipped on her own sunglasses. "Shrimp cocktail for lunch, hope that's okay."

"Sounds good."

Hell, he would have eaten raw fish if it meant he could sit here and look at her. The soft curves of her shoulders were pale pink from the sun, like the inside of a shell. A shadow shot down from her collarbone, narrowing at her cleavage, creating a perfect triangle against her white, creamy skin. She flicked her hair from her shoulders.

"How about a glass of wine? Or would you like something with a little more punch?"

"How about just some punch. I don't like to drink while I'm working."

She gave him an odd look, as if she thought he was joking. Cleary wondered if Nick had said something to her about his brother's drinking. Probably not. Nick hadn't been one to mix private matters with business.

Lane asked Teresa for a glass of wine and a soft drink, and a couple of minutes later the drinks and two large plates of shrimp cocktail were set in front of them. The sun warmed Cleary's back and, behind it, came the faintest breeze, a breath of air, as if someone were blowing softly against his neck. "You spend much time out here?" he asked her.

"Not this summer. No." She speared a piece of shrimp, washed it down with a sip of wine. "Buddy said he was redecorating the place for me. As a surprise, see. I was supposed to stay away until it was done. Things kept getting delayed, he said, and every time I asked it was always going to be another week. Finally I got suspicious one day, and drove out here."

She took another bite of her lunch, and Cleary waited for her to continue. "I got here and found Buddy's car parked next to a pink Cadillac. It didn't look like the kind of car a construction worker would be driving, so I parked down the road and walked back along the beach. I spotted Buddy sitting on the deck with a woman."

"What'd you do?"

"Oh, contemplated all the usual things: racing up there and making a scene, throwing rocks at them, whatever." She shrugged. "But I've never been one for making a scene, so I left before he saw me."

"That was when you hired Nick?"

"I waited another week, until Buddy told me there would be more delays at the beachhouse."

"Why didn't you just confront him, and get it out in the open?"

"That would have been fine with some men, but not with Buddy. I was feeling a gulf between us, and I didn't want to see our marriage slowly deteriorate into divorce. I knew that if I told I'd seen him with a woman, he could have easily made up some story about it being someone in the record business he was entertaining, and there was nothing to it. I wanted to present him with the facts, then give him a chance to patch things up."

Cleary sipped at his ginger ale, wondering why Williams—why any man—would double-time a looker like Lana. He had been in an alcoholic haze when Nick had pointed out Williams at the Crescendo Club, but not so drunk that he hadn't noticed that Williams was sure lacking in the looks department. He was the sort of man who no doubt had bought his women, and money was probably the main reason Lana had married him.

"Were you in love with him?"

She set her wineglass down, and smiled. "It wasn't a great passionate affair, if that's what you're wondering. But, I'm a woman who believes that once you make up your mind and get yourself hitched, you should keep the knot tied. So yeah, in my way I loved him."

He nodded without commenting.

"I suppose you think that's an old-fashioned idea. But that's the way I feel." She tipped her sunglasses back into her hair. "You married, Mr. Cleary?"

"Separated, and definitely headed for a divorce."

"Did you make any effort to reconcile?"

Cleary wasn't here to talk about his personal life. He didn't see any reason to spill his guts about drinking. Or about anything else, for that matter.

"I didn't hire anyone to spy on her, if that's what you mean."

"I wasn't implying that you did." She seemed embarrassed now. "Sorry, I didn't mean to pry, Mr. Cleary," she said with a serious look.

He shrugged. "Call me Jack, all right?"

They finished their lunch, saying little of consequence, each one taking care not to trespass into the mine fields of the other's past. Yet, Cleary knew that if he was going to work for Lana, he needed to penetrate into her relationship with Buddy. The problem, of course, was how to do it without raising her suspicions that he had reasons of his own for taking this case. He didn't see any need at this point for her to know that Nick's death was related to the Williams case.

"Would you like any dessert, Jack?"

"No thanks. Could I see the house?"

"Sure. C'mon, I'll give you the tour."

They entered the living room through a sliding glass door. In fact, the entire wall that faced the ocean was glass. There was a bar along one wall and a decor that was definitely not castoffs from the other house. The pine floor shone, and the air smelled clean and new, just like everything in the room.

Clean, new, and expensive. "What got decorated? This place looks fine just like it is."

"Oh, Buddy kept his word. This is all new."

To the tune of how much? he wondered.

"By the way, I'm going to need a list of friends and associates, people who saw your husband on a regular basis." He paused a moment. "That includes the names of the women who Buddy was seeing."

"I'm afraid I can't be of much help. You see Buddy protected me from his business dealings, and everyone associated with them. I guess you could say he held me up on a pedestal, or so I thought. As far as the names of the women, you'll have to get them from the tapes. Nick hadn't given me much as far as specific names."

"Who'd the pink Cadillac belong to?"

"I don't know."

She motioned for him to follow and showed him the rest of the house—a contemporary kitchen, a guest bedroom, a maid's room, and the master bedroom. It was done in pale blues, blues the color of ice, with a large bed that dominated the room. Lana pulled open the drapes, revealing another magnificent view of the Pacific. "This was one of the rooms your brother bugged." She glanced toward the bed, and turned away.

He could imagine what goodies Nick must've gotten on tape in here.

"What other rooms did he bug, do you know?"

"The living room," she said, walking back into it.

"What about the maid? Was she around all that time?"

Lana shook her head. "No. I didn't hire her until after Buddy was killed, and then only because I was reluctant to stay out here alone at night."

She pivoted, as if looking for something, and raked her fingers through her hair as she walked over to a sunny nook in the corner and sat on the wide, cushioned ledge below the windows. She opened them; a warm, salt-swollen breeze rushed into the room. She leaned back, the breeze ruffling her hair. He stopped next to her, leaned over next to her to look out the window. He was close enough to catch the faint fragrance of salt on her skin and the vestige of perfume.

"This has always been my favorite spot in the house, because it catches the morning sun. I like having my coffee here, especially on days when it's sunny and cool out."

Interesting, Cleary thought, running his hand over the windowsill. A part of a label was still on the window, and the frame looked new. So did the floor. Yet, she was talking like the nook had always been here. He didn't know what that meant, and was about to ask when he reconsidered. He filed it away with bits and pieces of other information, his head a sea of trivia and facts that might or might not connect in the future.

"Feel like a swim?" she asked suddenly.

He looked down at himself and laughed. "I'm not exactly dressed for it."

"No problem. I'm sure there's a pair of swimming trunks around here somewhere." She touched him, fingers cool and soft against his arm. He hoped it wasn't his imagination that her hand lingered longer than was necessary. "Let's have a look, hmm?"

They returned to the bedroom and she opened a bottom drawer of the bureau. "I put a lot of Buddy's stuff in here until I could decide what to do with it." Her long fingers lifted shirts, socks. "Oh, wait a minute. Maybe I put the trunks in the closet."

If it had been dark, Cleary would have hit the Pacific as naked as a newborn. Lana went over to the closet, lifting up on the balls of her feet and patting around on an upper shelf. Just then, the phone rang. She hurried across the room to answer it.

"Hello? . . . Oh, yes, sure, he's here." She covered the receiver with her hand. "It's for you, Jack. It's your secretary."

Damn, just when things were getting interesting. He reached for the receiver. "Dottie?"

She was talking fast and furiously, as if she were in a hurry, maybe en route to a tryout at Paramount. "Sorry to cut in on your clambake, Cleary, but the lab just delivered some surveillance photos Nick had taken at Williams's beachhouse last week. You'll never guess who he's got coming out the front door."

Just say it, Dottie. But no, now they were playing guessing games. Okay. "Who is it?"

"The guy on the radio, the Gator. I recognized him right away. I've seen him at the clubs."

"I'll be right there."

T E N

Air Waves

A crowd of teenagers was milling about as Cleary entered the lobby of KGFJ. In one corner, dressed penguin style, a doo-wop group practiced their harmonies. There was also a Gene Vincent clone in the crowd, and a squeaky-clean, penny-loafered crew quartet. As he waited to talk to the receptionist, he watched the groups avidly performing for each passing DJ or record-company type.

The receptionist, a young man dressed in a mohair suit and a Milano collar, was deeply engrossed in conversation on the phone. A personal call, Cleary thought. Finally he leaned over the desk, and spoke into the man's ear. "I need to see Mr. Baytor."

"I'm sorry, but Mr. Baytor's not available. He's on the air." Then he flashed an acrid smile, dismissing him.

Cleary was unperturbed. "It's important that I see him," he said. "We've got some business to discuss."

"Not now you don't," the receptionist said, then took his hand off the receiver of the phone. "I don't care if it's Queen Isabella of Denmark's birthday, I am not wearing a Davy Crockett cap," he said to whoever was on the phone. Now his eyes widened. "Fine! Forget it, Adrian! Cancel the marshmallows, cancel the balloons, cancel—"

Cleary's hand slammed down over the button on the phone's cradle, disconnecting the call. Then he calmly took the receiver out of the receptionist's hand and hung it up. "Don't you know it's rude to talk on the phone when someone's trying to ask you something?" He smiled. "Now. Where do I find Baytor?"

"Well, excuse me for living, Atilla," the man responded, "but you do not have an appoint—"

"My manager givin' you a rough ol' ride?" a voice cut in from behind Cleary.

He turned to see Johnny Betts approaching with a guitar case, two-tone bucks, and a traffic-stopping Eddie Cochran rockabilly suit.

Reaching the desk, he slapped Cleary soundly on the back. "All those late hours, eh Hoss?" Betts grinned at the receptionist. "Name's Eddie Burnett. I'm a slice early for my live gig with the Gator."

Forgetting Cleary, the receptionist beamed at

Betts. "Oh, yes. We've been promoting it on the air all afternoon. Have you heard it?"

"I'm hep," Betts said with a grin, then winked at Cleary, who looked distinctly unamused.

The receptionist pushed the desk buzzer, unlocking a nearby "Personnel Only" door, and pointed the way.

A moment later, Cleary was striding down the long corridor with Betts on his heels, lugging the guitar case. "You don't hear too well, do you, Betts?" he said, glancing over his shoulder.

"Say what?" He cupped his ear, then bent over laughing. "If I did, you'd still be jitterbugging with Tinkerbell back there. You got no finesse, Jack. Your brother had finesse. It's something you gotta work on."

"Well, I hope you can get your money back on the costume rental 'cause I'm not auditioning this week," he snapped as he continued down the corridor.

"Costume rental!" he shouted after him. "Hey, man, I own these threads."

Cleary spotted Bobby Baytor through a window, seated in his broadcast booth before a large hanging microphone. As in the surveillance photo of him, the Gator wore a distinctive goatee. He was garbed in a long-sleeved Banlon shirt and shades that would blot out the afterburner of an F-14.

He pushed his way into the booth, and heard the Mad Rapper spewing a string of words Cleary hardly recognized as English as he cued up a 45 on his console turntable and leaned into the mike. "... This ain't no hoot. This ain't no nanny. The Gator came to rock and the Gator's got your granny! Yooooooowwww! Chomp, chomp, chomp!!"

Then he assumed a relatively human-sounding voice, and added, "This KGFJ groove goes out to Charleeene from Nicky... 'Ooooooooooby Dooby' by Rooooy the big O Orbison!!"

As the music kicked in, Baytor switched off his mike, and spun around. He glanced at the clock on the wall, then at Cleary and Betts. "Who're you?"

"I'm here to ask you about Buddy Williams. What was your connection?"

Baytor stared at him, his expression changing from mild annoyance to anger. "How did you...? Get out. I'm on the air. I don't have to answer any damn questions."

"This won't take long if you cooperate."

He jabbed a finger at Cleary. "You are trespassing, man," he hissed, then suddenly lurched for the phone to call security. Getting no dial tone, he shot a beleaguered look over at Cleary, who held the frayed end of the phone line he'd ripped out of the wall.

"That's not answering my question, Baytor. Next time it'll be your goddamn neck that gets yanked. Now start talking, pal."

"I don't know diddly 'bout any Williams. Now if ya don't mind, I got a show to do."

Betts, posted by the lone exit of the cramped room, was leafing through a stack of 45s, and, to Cleary's chagrin, reacted aloud to each and every one of his musical faves. Cleary ignored him, and moved in closer to Baytor. He slid off the man's sunglasses.

"Take a look," he said, tossing a surveillance photo

taken at Williams's beachhouse, onto Baytor's desk. "See the little man with the goatee? Looks just like you, doesn't it? I'd even swear it was you. Out at the beach catching some rays, working on your tan, no doubt. And working on something else, too. Right Baytor?"

"Get lost."

"That beachhouse of his was wired to the gills; every last conversation was taped."

Baytor pushed away the photo as if trying to distance himself from the evidence. He was beginning to look acutely uncomfortable. Beads of sweat pimpled his brow. The song ended, and he flipped the 45 over and cued it up on the turntable without comment.

"Now you can talk to me about Williams, or to my friends downtown," Cleary continued. "They're always up for a good payola story from a celebrity speed freak."

Betts looked up at Cleary, surprised by his wealth of information, then shook his head mournfully at Baytor. "As a charter member of your fan club, Gator, I am mortified, man, just mortified."

Cleary shot Betts a look, silencing him.

"You got proof I was selling airplay, pal? If you do, I'd like to see it."

Cleary leaned closer to him. "How 'bout I just beat the living crap outa you instead? How would that be, Mr. Gator? More to your liking?"

Baytor held up his hands, palms out. "Hey, be cool, man. I don't know zip about that bon voyage Buddy got, honest. And that's the Gator truth of the matter."

"That's what bothers me," Cleary responded, dryly. "Maybe you could tell me who he worked for."

"Starlite Records."

"Get serious. I can read the papers. Give me a human dimension, Baytor."

He shrugged. "How should I know, man. Do I look like the *Encyclopaedia Britannica*?"

Cleary leaned over, picked up Baytor's sunglasses, and snapped them in two. He tossed the pieces onto Baytor's desk. "Next, your eyes, pal," and he grabbed Baytor by the collar and drew a fist back.

"All right. Guy name of Mickey Schneider signs the checks, whatever that tells you. That's all I know. Believe me, that's all."

He glanced at the Orbison record, which was almost over. "If I don't get back on the air, we're going to have lots of company."

Cleary let go of his shirt and Baytor fell back against the chair. As the refrain of the song ended, Cleary strode toward the door.

Betts stepped forward, placing a 45 on Baytor's desk. "To Rhonda from Johnny, Gator. The B side."

Cleary emerged from the KGFJ building into the warm night, and headed down Sunset on foot. Betts, jazzed from the confrontation in the booth, was hard on Cleary's heels, lugging his guitar case.

"Man, talk about casual. You played the Gator back there like a freakin' minuet." He bumped Cleary accidentally with the case. "I mean, how'd you know he was an amphetamine hype with a payola bankroll?"

Cleary glanced back, his annoyance as stubborn as

an itch. "He's a ten-grand-a-year record spinner with"
—he jerked his thumb toward the KGFJ parking
lot—"a Packard Caribbean, record-promoter play-
mates, and pupils the size of caraway seeds." He
shrugged. "I filled in the blanks."

Visibly impressed, Betts paused on the sidewalk.
"All right, *Sherlock!*" He hurried after him. "So where
do we go from here?"

Cleary stopped dead in his tracks, turned, and
looked Betts square in the eye. "*We* are going nowhere. *We* have seen the last of each other."

Frustrated, Betts rolled his eyes at the skyline in a
classic "what a drag" look. "Talk about looking a gift
horse in the tonsils, Cleary. I mean, listen up a minute, will ya, man?"

Cleary, who was about to turn away, pointed a
finger at Betts. "No, *you* listen up, mister. I'm sure
you're a regular Boy Scout beneath all the tattoos and
Brylcreem, but I've got serious work cut out for me,
and the last thing I need in my rearview right now is
some thrill-crazy, rock-and-roll delinquent with a
'Blackboard Jungle' wardrobe, a nightmare for a car,
and a haircut that needs a building permit. You got it
straight?"

He glared at Betts, who jabbed his hands in his
tight black jeans and hunched his shoulders. Cleary
turned on his heels and continued down the sidewalk
toward the side street where he'd parked his Caddy.

Betts stood there a moment, wondering whether to
take it personally. As he drew in a deep breath and
slowly let it out in a disgruntled sigh, his peripheral
vision gradually registered the approach of a familiar

'56 Packard 400 turning onto Sunset from a side street. As the car slowly approached Cleary from behind, Betts saw a split-second flash of neon careen off a slowly raised metallic object in the passenger window.

Sensing what was about to happen, Betts shouted Cleary's name, the sound cutting through the pea-soup-thick night air. Cleary figured Betts was about to curse him, and ignored the warning yell.

Betts took off at full sprint down the sidewalk, his two-tone bucks pounding the pavement, the sound echoing in his ears. As he ran, he flipped open the guitar case, dropping it as he grabbed the barrel of a sawed-off shotgun.

Cleary glanced back just as Betts hit him with a running, broadside tackle. He tumbled to the ground and was about to roll over and grab Betts by the throat when he heard a volley of gunfire shatter the windows over his head. Shards of glass sprayed over him as the bullets tore into the fashionably dressed mannequins inside the Sy Devore haberdashery. The mannequins folded, disintegrated in an explosion of plaster, mohair, and highboy collars. Instinctively Cleary assumed a crouched firing position just in time to get off two rounds at the quickly accelerating Packard. Beside him, Betts fired the sawed-off.

As the car disappeared down the boulevard, a few terrified citizens peered cautiously out of nearby storefronts. Cleary rose shakily to his feet, brushed off his coat, glanced at Betts. The kid looked about, then discreetly slipped the sawed-off into the custom-designed sling inside his sport coat.

"Serious work is right." He threw a look at Cleary. "Later, C-man." He headed back down the boulevard, slowing a moment to pick up the guitar case.

When Cleary recovered his voice, he yelled, "Hey, Betts."

But Betts was ignoring him. The kid closed the guitar case, then glanced over his shoulder as Cleary walked up to him. "You calling, man?"

Say it, man, Cleary chastised himself. *Just spit it out*. He finally extracted the words with about as much ease as he would his own teeth.

"Putting aside your taste in clothes and music, and the fact that I need a UN translator to understand you half the time...I mean, just for the sake of discussion..." Running out of words, a pained grimace contorted his face. "Oh, screw it. C'mon, we got work to do, Betts."

Restored of his sense of dignity, Betts stood his ground just long enough to run a back pocket comb coolly through his styled do. Then, with a shake of his head at the man's total lack of eloquence, he accepted Cleary's offer. "All right, Mr. Personality."

He sauntered after his reluctant mentor, their implausible alliance forged under gunfire.

ELEVEN

Starlite

As a newspaper delivery truck pulled away from the Starlite Record Building and onto a vacant street, Cleary eased away from the curb, drove the Eldorado around to the back of the building, and parked it in a dark corner with a view of the street. It was just before dawn, and he cut short a yawn with his palm.

"You think you can handle the lock on that door?" he said, motioning toward the rear entrance.

"Piece of cake," Betts answered, though he was too far away to even see the lock. "You ready? Let's go?"

"Just wait a minute."

"Wait? Wait for what? We already waited fifteen minutes across the street."

"Let's have a little chat." Something in Cleary's tone clued Betts that he was rubbing him the wrong way. "Where you from, Johnny?"

"Outside Memphis."

"How'd you meet Nick?"

"Through a probation officer. See, I ran into a little trouble after I first got out here."

"What kind of trouble?"

"I was caught with my hands in a cash register."

"Too lazy to get a job?"

"Thought I'd save some time. That's all past, though. Your brother turned me around."

"Yeah. I can see that."

"I mean, you know, I haven't gone out and done anything stupid. Except for maybe the night at the courthouse."

"Where you get your money?"

Betts threw him a look that said back off. "I pick up jobs here and there, and Nick paid me. What is this, 'The Sixty-Four Thousand Dollar Question'?"

Cleary met Johnny's eyes. "I like to know who I'm working with."

"Yeah, well you go about it like a cop," he said, with a touch of defiance.

Cleary looked away.

"Guess there's a reason for that, huh?" Betts said in a softer voice, realizing he'd hit a nerve.

Cleary nodded noncommittally, then pointed out to the street as a patrol car eased by. "Let's wait one more minute to make sure he keeps going. If he comes back you're a singer from out of town. I'm your manager. We drove all night, and just arrived for your audition."

"Sounds cool," he said, drumming the dashboard.

Cleary glanced at his watch, waited. "All right. Let's do it."

Buoyed with confidence, Betts took the lead, and in less than a minute jimmied the lock on the back door. Inside, it took him just thirty seconds to open an office door that said, MICKEY SCHNEIDER—PRESIDENT.

As Cleary circled around Schneider's desk, Betts stopped to gaze appreciatively at a gold record hanging on the wall. "Dig it, man, Donnie Hammond." He tilted each of the framed records and photographs on the wall looking for a safe. Then he moved on to the file cabinet.

Cleary pulled open the desk drawers, rummaged through them in the dim light. Then he tried the doors of a heavy wooden cabinet behind Schneider's desk, and found them locked.

"I'll get it," Betts offered. Pulling out a slender, hairpinlike tool from his shirt, he jimmied the lock. A moment later, he smiled up at Cleary. "Magic."

Cleary opened the cabinet door and reached inside. As he did, he knocked over a decanter of Scotch, spilling it on his pants. "Damn." He set the container upright, and brushed a hand over his pant leg. "Just a liquor cabinet."

He was about to close the door when he noticed a ledger resting upright against the cabinet wall on the left. He flicked his lighter on and began paging through it. The lighter Nick had given him. There was a certain irony about that, he thought, as he turned through several more pages.

"So we were waiting out there for the local cop to go by," Betts said as he rifled the files. "Was that it?"

Cleary didn't answer.

"I guess your experience as a cop is paying off," Betts said.

When Cleary again didn't respond, he continued, "Nick told me you got a raw deal. Someone set you up on a bribery rap."

"Betts, stick to your business over there."

"All right. All right. But I don't see anything labeled 'payoffs.' What do you think it would be under?"

"Keep looking," he growled.

"Wish we could turn on the lights."

Cleary shook his head, exasperated with Betts, then leaned forward, staring at the page before him. "You read?"

Betts looked up. "Menus."

"Check this out."

Cleary handed him the ledger, opened to the page he had been studying, then flipped him the lighter. Betts turned on his reading light, and leaned close to the page.

"Hey, the Clovers never went gold with that song." He stabbed his finger at the page. "Says here they shipped half a million platters of 'Lovey Dovey,' and I know for a fact they topped out on the charts with half that."

Cleary frowned, moved up to Betts, and planted his finger on the opposite page. "Try over here. There's two pages to this menu."

"Jeez, there must be at least two hundred grand in payoffs," Betts said after a moment. He looked up, pocketing Cleary's gold lighter. "And all to our favorite radio personalities, including fifty Gs to our buddy, the Gator."

Cleary noticed a stack of cards on one corner of Schneider's desk and picked one off it. It was an unposted invitation to a party. Something about it stirred his attention, but he couldn't pinpoint it, so he pocketed the card. "Let's get out of here." He took back the ledger, ripped out the page, and returned it to the desk drawer.

"Put it back, Betts."

"Put what back?" he asked.

Cleary walked over to him and began frisking him. "Hey," Betts shrieked. "We don't know each other that well, man."

Cleary pulled the gold record out from under the back of Betts's T-shirt, and hung it on the wall again. Next to it he noticed a picture of two men; one he pegged as Schneider, the other looked like a reformed mobster.

"I don't feel like getting popped on the way home 'cause some hillbilly klepto's filling out his record collection. You got that?"

"Klepto, huh?" His body stiffened in a defensive stance, his mouth turned down angrily. "Hey, I may be a lot of things, Cleary, but a sexual pervert ain't one of 'em. You better dig that from the hip-hop if you want to keep working with me."

They left the office without another word, and were about to leave the building when Betts turned to

Cleary. "And another thing. I don't jus' wanna know the name of the song, I want the lyrics, too."

"What the hell are you talking about?" Cleary asked, wondering what he was doing in the same postal zone with this preverbal delinquent.

"About what we're doing. That's what. I wanna know what's going on."

"All right." He motioned toward the door. "Out."

It was dawn as they drove away from the Starlite Building, and traffic was just starting to pick up. Betts looked expectantly at Cleary. "Well, man, speak up."

"About what?"

Betts folded his arms and stared out the window, irked by Cleary's strong, silent-guy game.

"Okay, Betts," Cleary began. "Get ready for a few lines of lyrics. Before Williams got knocked off, he was about to spill his guts to a federal task force about the Mafia's attempt to control the record biz through payola schemes. Mickey Schneider had everything to lose if he talked."

Betts nodded, pleased that Cleary was taking him into his confidence.

"Now here's something for you to think about. Both Nick's office and my apartment were tossed after Nick was killed. Whoever the guys in the Packard were, they didn't get all they wanted when they got the tapes."

Betts shrugged. "Maybe Nick didn't hand over both sets."

"There was more than one?"

He nodded as they turned on Sunset. "I'm sure he

made duplicates, for insurance I s'pose, though it beats me where he would've stashed 'em."

"That's it," Cleary said softly, hitting the heel of his hand against the steering wheel. Several blocks slipped by as he mulled over what to do next.

"You can drop me right on the corner. I've got the Merc in the body shop down the block. Trying out a new color after our little run the other night."

"I think you better park it a while. You need more than a paint job to hide that thing."

"It's my wheels, man."

"It's your ass, too." Cleary pulled to the curb. "I've got something to keep you occupied."

"Yeah, what?" Betts asked suspiciously, the long hours starting to show in his impatience.

"I want you to pay Schneider a visit."

"And say what? 'I like your gold records'?"

"Tell him you were with Nick the night he got hit. Tell him you've got the Buddy Williams tapes."

"That's gonna make me a real popular boy. I like it. Want me to quote a figure on the tapes?"

"Ask for ten grand."

"Nice round figure." Betts placed his hand on the door handle.

"By the way, where'd you learn to pick locks like that?"

"Home-study course." He grinned and pushed open the door. "See you later, C-man."

Cleary drove off, feeling as if the night's work had been productive. Schneider was definitely in deep, but was he the end of the trail? He slowed for a traffic light, and as he came to a stop, remembered the invitation he had taken from Schneider's desk. He pulled it out of his coat pocket, and reread it.

Starlite Records requests the pleasure of your company in honor of their newest recording artist, Eddie Burnett.

The last line announced that the party would be held at the residence of Eddie Rosen. Cleary stared at the name. Something about it bothered him. He didn't know the man, but knew he didn't like him. He wanted to find out what Rosen's connection was with Schneider and Starlite. He pocketed the invitation as the light changed.

Cleary drove on, but when he reached the turnoff for St. Ives, he kept going. He headed out of town, intent on taking a look at Rosen's house. But somewhere en route his mind drifted from lack of sleep. He made a wrong turn and didn't realize it, not until he reached a familiar street. He couldn't believe it. His mind had gone on automatic, and he had been drawn like a magnet to his old house in the suburbs, to Ellen.

In the pale morning light, the place looked smaller than he remembered—a pale yellow concrete house set back in a thicket of trees. Ellen had landscaped the yard with hedges and cactuses and wildflowers. And for a long time, it had been their private Eden, a world sliced away from his life on the streets. And then he had blown it.

He parked parallel to the edge of the yard and got

out of the Eldorado. He strolled up the walk, remembering other mornings when he had done exactly this, mornings after working around the clock, when he was so beat he could barely see straight. He had unlocked the door and stepped into the silent house, embracing its warmth and the faint fragrance of Ellen's perfume that lingered in the air like the scent of fresh flowers. The first thing he had done was shower, scrubbing away the vestiges of the L.A. streets. And then he had slipped into the bedroom, into Ellen's arms.

Gone, buddy. All of it down the tubes.

He rang the doorbell. When she didn't answer, he knocked and rang the bell again and again. As the door finally opened, his heart flopped in his chest, and then there she was, standing there in a short terry-cloth robe, her black hair tangled, her eyes puffy from sleep. She just gazed at him for a long moment, a hand holding the throat of the robe closed, as if she expected him to rip it away.

"You gotta be drunk to be here. Right? You're drunk, aren't you, Jack? I can smell it on you." She started to slam the door, but his shoe jutted out, wedged between the door and the jamb.

"I'm not drunk, Ellen. I just want to talk to you." He pushed the door open.

She stood slightly behind it, her dark eyes glossy with anger—and perhaps a bit of fear, as well. She ran her fingers through her hair, combing it back. "Make it snappy."

"Thanks for coming to Nick's funeral."

The anger immediately bled out of her face. "Oh,

God," she whispered. "I'm sorry about Nick. I really am. I—I wanted to say something to you that day, but..."

"But you were with some other guy. Some cowboy actor, right?"

Now why the hell had he said that? The anger leaped back into her eyes. "So what about it?"

"Who is he?"

"A friend of mine."

"A lover, you mean."

She didn't answer.

Cleary, his voice harder, insistent, a voice that demanded an answer, said, "A lover. Right? Does he wear his spurs to bed, Ellen?"

"Jack, correct me if I'm wrong, but we're separated, right? You were drunk, remember? You got suspended from your job, and for weeks you made my life a hell. I put up with all of it until you hit me. Now if you don't mind, I'd like to go back to bed."

He dry-washed his face with his hands. "I'm sorry, I didn't mean—"

"You never do," she snapped. "You always mean so well, don't you, Jack? But then you somehow have this way of twisting things, making things so—so ugly."

Was it true?

Was he the sort of man who ranted and raged and then apologized later? When he was sober? *You were worse, buddy. Much worse.* "Look couldn't we have coffee or lunch or something, Ellen? Couldn't we at least try to—"

"No. You had plenty of chances, Jack. We tried,

and nothing worked. Now please. Just go. Don't make me call the cops. I really don't want to. But if you don't leave, I will. I swear I will."

Cleary slid his foot out of the door. He reached out and touched the back of his hand to her face. Then he turned and moved back down the walk, an ache wider than the Pacific tearing open inside him. *Call me back, Ellen. C'mon. Please say, "Hey, Jack, hold on." C'mon, just say it.*

But she didn't. He heard the door closing, softly.

She's nice enough and she's sure a looker, Jack, but I don't know, man, I think she's gonna break your heart, Nick had once said to him shortly after Cleary and Ellen had gotten married.

Break your heart. Yeah, you bet. Too bad it turned out to be true.

His legs felt wooden as he started back down the walk. He heard the whisper of his own footfalls against the concrete, whispers like a small, lost voice, the voice of the man he had been.

Somewhere distant, a bird warbled in the stillness, as if willing him to glance back. He did. And there, silhouetted in the bedroom window, was a man, watching him. He knew, without knowing how he knew, that it was the actor.

◆◆◆◆◆◆◆◆

T W E L V E

Studio Work

"Mr. Schneider, please," Johnny Betts said in his most polite, adult tone to the secretary who answered the telephone at Starlite Records.

He was at a phone booth just three blocks away from the record company, and figured Mickey Schneider would quickly fit him into his schedule when he heard what the call was about.

"Mr. Schneider is going to be busy all day at a recording session. Can I take a message?"

"Yes. Ah, I mean, no," Betts stuttered. "Maybe you can help me. I'm supposed to fill in for the recording engineer. But I didn't get the address of the studio."

"Well, you certainly shouldn't be bothering Mr. Schneider about that. I'll tell you where it is."

Betts jotted the address on the inside of the phone booth as she gave it to him. "Thanks. You're a doll. I just hit the buzzer to get in, right?"

"If the band's practicing, you might not be heard for a while. It's better to go around to the side, and press the lever just over the door and let yourself in."

Now why couldn't all secretaries be so helpful? he thought with a smile. Then he hung up and started thumbing a ride to the studio. He had conceded that Cleary was probably right about the Mercury. Even with a new color, the cops might still recognize it.

A half hour later, Betts was leaning against the wall in the corner of the recording studio, looking passive and indifferent. But inside he was revved. What luck, what hot damn luck. Eddie Burnett, the *numero uno* ticket in town, was right here cutting a new tune.

This was something he could tell his kids about. His grandkids. It would become one of those stories the family passed down from generation to generation. *Your grandpa Betts was there the day Eddie Burnett recorded "Sunset Strip." He even talked to him, got to know him. They were buddies back then. Grandpa Betts even got in a lick or two with the band from time to time.*

Eddie struck the first chord of the song, played a couple of bars, then stopped. He leaned over to the stand-up bass player, told him the chord change. He counted to three, and they hit it again.

Betts glanced across the studio at Schneider, who

was fidgeting about next to a blonde half his age. It was obvious he didn't have a clue to what was happening onstage, but he could smell money in the making. Schneider, he figured, was the type that would applaud someone farting if he could make a fast buck on it.

He turned back to the band. Cleary would be blowing a fuse if he knew he was more interested in Burnett than Schneider. But when it came to music Cleary was like Nick; he was deaf. The sounds that made his soul sing, that made the world something more than the usual drag, were just noise to people like Cleary who didn't know how to listen, who didn't feel it. But there wasn't another place he would rather be right now. Rock and roll was a tidal wave, and Eddie B. was ridin' high. He would just take his time getting around to talkin' to Schneider, because once he laid his rap on him, there was no more hangin' out here.

After a few bars of the song, Burnett signaled the band to stop again. Schneider stood up and took a couple of steps toward Burnett to find out if he liked what he had been hearing.

"What d'ya think, Eddie?"

"It's not working."

"'It's not working,'" Schneider said, throwing up his hands. "The damn thing doesn't work!"

Betts knew that for Burnett, this was just part of getting the tune right, but Schneider looked like he was on the edge of despair. He was just probably thinking Burnett was about to throw in the towel, to tell him the song was "broke." That would be the end of it. Schneider wouldn't have a clue how to fix it.

He turned to his girlfriend, a store-bought blonde who affected a Monroe look. She was sitting on a high stool, her legs crossed at the knees, filing her red-painted nails. "What's wrong with it?" he asked her.

"I like it," she replied, without glancing up from her nails.

"Hey, just fix your goddamn nails, will you please? And keep your mouth shut. This is a professional recording studio, got that?"

She shrugged, and kept filing.

"Whyn't you try the chord change like on 'Locomotive'?" Betts asked.

"Oh, here's another freaking country heard from," Schneider snapped, then looked to Burnett to see his reaction.

"That could work," Eddie said, nodding thoughtfully. "Damn, it just might."

"Yeah? You think it can?" Schneider gushed. Then he took Betts's suggestion as his own. "See, I'm wondering if that could be it. You know, I think it might now that I think about it. Kind of like 'Locomotive.'"

No one's gonna believe this, Betts thought. No one was going to believe that he, Johnny Betts, had told Eddie Burnett the chord change he needed to make "Sunset Strip" work. Not even his grandkids would swallow that.

Schneider, a wide smile on his face, moved over to Betts, and pointed at him. "Where do I know you from? You're with... Who the hell are you with now? It's right on the tip of my tongue."

"Me, myself, and I."

As quickly as Schneider turned on, he turned off. "Uh-huh. I'll tell you we're a little busy here right now. You better move on."

"I've got a demo I think you'll be interested in, Mr. Schneider."

"See, we really aren't signing anybody new this week. Got that?"

"You don't want to miss this one, Mickey. It's called 'Buddy Williams Live at Home.' It's his final performances. Got *that*?"

Schneider frowned at Betts, then looked around as if he were missing something. He crooked a finger at Betts. "You follow me."

He led him into a recording booth. He stabbed a thumb over his shoulder and told the recording engineer seated at the console to get out.

The man tapped his watch. "Studio time, Mickey. The clock doesn't stop."

"Right, get out of here."

The engineer shook his head, and walked out. *I guess I really am replacing the engineer*, Betts thought, and smiled to himself at the irony. Schneider checked to make sure all the mikes were off, then turned to Betts, who was casually tapping a Lucky against Cleary's gold lighter.

"I don't know what you're talking about, kid. What's this all about?"

Betts swept his arm out, indicating his surroundings. "Nice of you to take all the time and trouble, Mickey. Mighty nice of you."

"I'm not kidding, wise guy. You tell whoever sent

you over here I got zero exposure in the Buddy Williams hit. You got that straight?"

"Fine. I thought you were a music lover, thought you'd appreciate having a chance to hear Williams's tunes." Betts started toward the door.

"Who sent you?"

"I'm a free agent, pal. I was riding with Nick Cleary the night he got wasted for the Williams tapes. Nick had me hold the originals. Not that you know what I'm talking about or anything."

"Just so I know, if anyone was interested, how much would you want for 'em?"

"Ten grand. Just so you know."

"You may want to call me at my office tomorrow in case I've heard something that might interest you."

"Gotcha."

Betts headed out the door, pausing in the outside studio to light his Lucky. He frowned as several flicks of the metal roller failed to produce a flame.

"Nice lighter, Cleary," he mumbled, then pulled off the casing. A small locker key fell into his palm. Betts studied it, noting the word "Union" on one side, and the number "19" on the other, then quickly put it back in the lighter, closed it up, and pocketed it.

Burnett, in midsong, apparently having solved his problem, nodded to him. "Later, man."

"Crazy," Betts said, and nodded back. His thoughts were already a hundred feet in front of him, focused on the key, the goddamn key.

Betts stood at the magazine rack in Union Station flipping through a copy of *Hot Rod* magazine. He had just spent two hours in the hot sun hitching a ride across town. He could've taken a bus, but he never took buses, and he wasn't going to start now. Looking at the magazine made him think about his Merc parked in the garage, ready and waiting. Forget this hitchhiking, and to hell with the cops. He was getting his wheels back this afternoon.

He gazed over the top of the magazine rack toward a row of lockers. Several sailors were standing in front of them as one of their buddies stuffed his duffel bag into one. Finally he inserted a coin, removed the key, and the white-clad sailors moved on.

Betts returned the magazine to the rack, and noticed the grizzled vendor eyeing him. "You don't want to do anything rash like pay for that?"

"Do I look stupid?"

"A man could starve," the vendor grumbled.

Betts ambled toward the row of lockers, taking out Cleary's lighter, and removing the key from it. He found number 19, and opened the locker. Inside was a metal suitcase labeled with tape on which had been written: "Buddy Williams Surveillance—Originals."

Damn. That's it. That says it all, Betts thought. He glanced over his shoulder, opened the case, and saw that it was full of reels. He quickly snapped the case closed. *Jeez. I've actually got them.*

He thought of his car again. He could get out of L.A., go to San Diego maybe, or north to San Francisco. Ten grand would go a long way. Opportunity wasn't just knocking, she was pounding, she was hammering, she was about to blow him away. For an instant, standing there with the case in his hand,

Betts imagined himself and Rhonda, sweet little Rhonda with those baby blues, sailing across the country in his Merc, with ten grand worth of dreams. Oh, Christ, but ten grand could take them a long way. Ten grand could get them to someplace like Montana. They could buy a ranch. Get married. Have kids. With ten grand, Johnny Betts could go legit.

He started walking, fast, through the bus station.

Ten grand. That was a stack of bills that would reach... how high? From the basin to the top of Mulholland Drive? To the moon?

Me and Rhonda... maybe a ranch... maybe a place on the beach. It sure sounded mighty tempting.

T H I R T E E N
The Party

The house, a Lautner-designed, futuristic monument to fast money, dominated an entire hilltop high above the city. Its circular driveway was congested with gleaming limos and luxury cars, red-jacketed parking valets, and arriving guests. It wasn't Cleary's kind of scene at all. Nick would have fit in better here. Nick had possessed a kind of chameleon quality, Cleary thought, that had enabled him to fit in just about anywhere, from the juke joints where the seedy lowlifes congregated, to the Malibu and Beverly Hills luaus of the wealthy, powerful, and famous. But Nick wasn't here, never would be, and for that very reason Cleary intended to make the best of it.

He parked the Eldorado across the street to avoid the valet parkers, then walked up to the immaculate residence. A cool slice of R&B was filtering into the sweltering night as he strolled up the walk in his expensive threads. His shoes were so new they squeaked.

He flashed his invitation to a burly, bald-headed man in a tuxedo standing near the door. The man glanced at the card and back at Cleary. He smiled and slapped him on the back. "Yeah. I got one, too. Come on in, join the party."

He tapped a finger at the invitation. "That's my boy. The guest of honor. Eddie's comin' on real strong. You seen him yet?"

Without waiting for an answer, he extended a hand, and pumped Cleary's arm. "Name's Narvel Husky, Eddie Burnett's manager. You in the industry, yourself, Mr. ah..."

"Cleary. Yeah, you bet I am. I'm a drummer. 'Scuse me." He walked past Husky into the room, trying to place the man's face.

"Hey, Cleary," Husky called after him. "You ought to meet Eddie's drummer, Jimmy."

Sure thing, pal.

It took him a couple of minutes, but he finally recalled that Husky and another man had been arguing at the Crescendo Club the night he had run into Nick. The night Williams was hit on his way out the door. Yeah, okay. He remembered now. It was one of the few things he could recall from his bender.

He meandered around the cavernous living room.

There were two crowded wet bars, a groaning Chasen's buffet, ultracontemporary furnishings, and a couple hundred mingling mob and Hollywood types with assorted arm pieces. The entire overdone spectacle was wrapped in floor-to-ceiling glass, which provided a stunning view of the well-lighted grounds and swimming pool, and the city below.

A waiter, moving through the crowd with a tray of drinks, offered one to Cleary. He was tempted to ask for a bourbon—his mouth was watering for one—but he wanted to keep a clear head tonight, and asked for a Coke instead.

"Sorry, not on this tray. Try the bar by the pool if you want it before the sun comes up," the man said, and moved on.

Cleary found the door and stepped out to the pool, a huge, kidney-shaped expanse of glowing aquamarine water. On one side was the glass wall of the house and the party within, and, on the other, the twelve million lights of the entire incandescent L.A. basin. He walked along the edge of the water to the poolside bar, and ordered his Coke. The bartender gave him a funny look, and Cleary figured he was probably the only teetotaler in the entire mob. Jesus, the irony.

To one side of the bar, under an overhanging palm frond, he noticed the back of a man as he spoke to a young woman in a sleazily seductive voice. "You see, behind every one of those beautiful L.A. lights is a house, or a car, and inside every one of those houses and cars is a...radio. It's kind of frightening when you think about it."

Cleary took a step closer and recognized Bobby Baytor, the Gator, dressed to seriously maim as he waxed eloquently to the pert-breasted and impressionable teen angel. The pretty little thing was clinging to his every word. "I mean the sheer power I have to influence the musical tastes of America's youth is an awesome responsibility. You see, I know what you kids are going through... Patsi." He slipped an arm around her. "It even keeps me awake some nights."

Right, Gator.

But the young thing laughed gaily, and Baytor's arm tightened around her. His eyes slid toward her generous cleavage. Then his unctuous smile faded as Cleary clamped a hand on his shoulder. Laughing bravely, he glanced from Cleary to the girl, then shook his head. "Amazing the people they let into these things."

When Cleary just continued staring at him, Baytor looked about uneasily, as if hoping someone would happen along and rescue him. Then he leaned toward the girl, bussed her on the cheek, and softly said, "The Gator loves you, honey. See you inside."

The girl smiled and drifted away, Gator gazing longingly after her. He reluctantly drew his eyes back to Cleary. "I told ya, pal, you got nothin' on me," he said, snapping his fingers and pointing at Cleary.

The finger, like the need for a bourbon, was a temptation for Cleary. He would've enjoyed snapping it like a matchstick. Instead, he looked around, confirming their relative privacy from the other guests who were strung along the pool patio like brightly colored lights. Then he turned back to Baytor. "Someone

I'm looking for is at this party. You're going to show me around. You're gonna be my tour guide, Gator."

Baytor laughed. "Yeah, right. Got any other fairy tales?"

He turned and started toward the house, but Cleary grabbed his arm and tightened his fingers like a vise. "Not so fast, pal." He pulled out the sheet from the ledger and held it in front of him. "Well, there's one about the fifty grand in payoffs Starlite Records gave this little pimp of a DJ. Think they'll let you up off your knees long enough to broadcast from Folsom, Bobby?"

Baytor turned pale and choked on an aspirated ice cube. When he recovered, he took Cleary's arm like a long, lost friend. "I see what you mean, buddy. Lemme buy you a drink, show you around. How would that be?" Under his breath, he added, "You're my cousin from Albany, anyone asks. Got that, man?"

Cleary grinned. "Let's hope no one asks."

Inside the house, at one end of the living room, a young black L.A. doo-wop group, in matching shawl-collar Madras jackets, was softly crooning the Clovers' "I've Got My Eyes on You." Baytor glanced around, then said, "There's Eddie Burnett, rookie of the week, right over there with a few of the Starlite boys." He pointed to his left.

Cleary spotted a young, pompadour-coiffed kid who reminded him of Johnny Betts. Next to him was Husky, who was introducing his somewhat dislocated rising star to a rabid pack of fast-talking record-industry types.

Baytor nodded to his right, where an overfed Westside shyster with a Palm Springs tan was surrounded by a brace of eye-shadowed Amazons. "That's Mickey Schneider's mouthpiece there in the charcoal mohair, partner in that new strip joint on Highland."

"Who are his friends with the hormone problems?"

"College-educated girls, and every one of them six feet and over. Go down to the joint some night and see them. Quite a show, I'll tell you."

Tall, smart strippers are just what L.A. needed, Cleary thought. He looked around, feeling a curious mix of amusement and repulsion at the overstated extravagance of the house and the people. But pure abhorrence gripped his gut at the abundant evidence that the Mafia influence in the record industry was now extensive. It only reinforced his need to locate the owner of the house, to check him out, assess him, figure out who and what and where.

"C'mon," Baytor said, leading him up a spiral staircase. Halfway up, he stopped and turned, a Tom Collins in one hand, and offered more insider gossip. "See the little, bald guy with his face in the martini? That's Peppy Roth. Used to be a big manager before all these melanons and hillbillies hit the charts."

He touched Cleary's arm. "Look over by the front doorway. That's the host himself, Eddie Rosen, shaking hands now. The guy next to him making the introductions is Mickey Schneider."

Cleary stared across the room from his perch. Rosen was in his late thirties, with a five-hundred-dollar Mainbocher suit and a short man's arrogance. He recognized Rosen and Schneider as the pair in the framed photograph that hung next to the gold records in Schneider's office. Now that he saw him in person he didn't like the man any better. Hell, now he knew his gut reaction to the man's name was no mistake. He was as sleazy as they came.

"What's his story?" Cleary asked.

"He just moved out here from the East Coast a year ago. He's associated with Starlite Records."

"Schneider's the president. So what's he do?"

"How should I know?" Baytor growsed. "I'm not the—"

"I know. You're not the *Encyclopaedia Britannica*," Cleary interrupted, then squeezed his arm. "But we've got a deal, Baytor, remember?"

"Okay, okay, man, I get the picture." He pulled his arm free. "He's a promoter, a wheeler-dealer. Top-level guy with lots of influential friends on the East Coast that you wouldn't want to mess with. You wouldn't want to mess with them here, either. That's all I know."

"Did things get too hot for him at home, or is he just expanding the family's sphere of influence? Or is there something else going on I should know about, huh, Gator?"

Baytor's mouth twitched and fussed. "What is this, 'Truth or Consequences'? Look, Cleary, aside from the occasional axle grease, I got no more to do with Starlite Records than the friggin' Pope. Now you mind if I mingle a little with the crowd, or you want people to think we're married?"

"Knock yourself out, Bobby."

Cleary descended the steps and headed toward one of the bars. It was time for a drink. He elbowed his way past Husky, who was being serenaded by a glad-handing PR hustler, and ordered a bourbon. As he waited for the bartender to pour it, he overheard the PR guy behind him. "Whattya talking about? No money? It's a chartbuster for chrissake, Narvel, and this kid of yours is pocketing twelve red-hot cents for every record that hits the street. *Twelve*. Count them."

Husky puffed on a cigar, pointed it at the man. "Amount of wax that hits the street and the amount that hits Starlite's books are two damn different things."

Cleary took a long draft of his bourbon, wincing as it burned a path down his throat. He considered the implication of what Husky had said, then turned to the PR man. "Guy knows how to throw a party, doesn't he?"

"Yeah, Rosen's a real comer," he replied, glancing over at Cleary.

"Hey, you met each other yet?" Husky asked. "This is Mr. Cleary. Don't think I caught your first name?"

"Jack," he said, and walked away.

Husky, who was semiloaded, turned to the PR man. "He's a drummer, a good one, too. Who'd you say you— Hey, where'd he go?"

"He don't look like no goddamn drummer that I've ever seen."

Cleary melted into the crowd, and found himself drawn outside to the pool again. He stared into the water, wondering if his first drink would lead to a second, and a third. If his thirst had returned, he would get a bottle on the way home. Another in the morning. Who cared? Certainly not Ellen. He knew that.

Sure. Start feeling sorry for yourself again, Cleary. See where that gets ya.

He caught a whiff of perfume as he realized someone had come up behind him.

"Hello there."

Cleary glanced over his shoulder, momentarily at a loss for words. Lana looked absolutely stunning in a sheer cocktail dress that hugged her in all the right places. Her thick, auburn hair was loose, falling to her shoulders in soft waves. Infinitely touchable hair, he thought. "Hello yourself. Surprised to see you here."

"That makes two of us."

"Thought I'd earn some of that money you gave me," he said quietly.

She nodded, meeting his critical gaze. Her husband had been in the ground for just over a week, and she was partying. He could see by the glaze in her eyes that she was half blitzed, and noticed that the drink in her hand had been drained to the ice cubes.

She averted her eyes as if reading his thoughts. "It gets a little lonely sitting out at that beachhouse," she said softly.

He thought—*hoped*—he wasn't imagining the wistfulness in her tone, a wistfulness that might've been an invitation. Then in a brisker, more business-like voice, she said, "Is there anything you need to tell me, Mr. Cleary? About Buddy?"

"Yeah." He smiled. "If the man had one ounce of good sense, he would have stayed home at night."

Color flushed Lana's cheeks, making her seem younger, more innocent, perhaps naive. "We never did get to take that swim the other day. Why don't you come out some afternoon, Jack?"

Now they were back to *Jack* instead of *Mr. Cleary*. He liked that. He liked the way she said his name, *Jack*, as if she were tasting it. "I mean, some day when it's unbearably hot in the city. Then we can take a swim and talk things over."

She stepped back as a young, good-looking hood approached with two fresh drinks in his hands. He handed one to Lana.

"C'mon baby, I want to show you something."

"Can it wait a second, Frankie?"

"Mickey's showing this slide with him and me in Acapulco. You gotta see it."

"I'll look at it in a minute."

"Look at it now." He touched her arm. Cleary watched the man's fat fingers tighten on her wrist. She shrugged and followed him, everything in her demeanor indicating that it was simply easier to go along than put up a fuss.

The hood didn't even consider the possibility that Cleary was a rival for Lana's attention. It grated on him, and he had to hold himself back from grabbing her by the arm and sinking his fist into the hood's mouth. Why did such a startlingly attractive and obviously bright woman keep company with a character like him?

Cleary was heading to the front door when he saw Rosen standing a few feet away with the Westside shyster and several of the Amazons. He walked over to him, wearing his most civilized smile.

"Mr. Rosen," he said, extending his hand, "just want to thank you for the party."

"Don't mention it." Rosen's expression was smug, the look of a man who knew he was king and that it was necessary to keep the peons in his kingdom happy by throwing a spread like this every so often. Then his expression changed. A nonplussed look claimed his features, as if he knew Cleary looked familiar, but couldn't place his face. "What'd you say your name was?" he asked, speaking up over the sound of the band, which had just segued into the Charms' "Heart of Stone."

He held back a moment, his eyes boring into Rosen's face. "Jack—Jack Cleary."

Something twitched deep in Rosen's eyes. Then he covered it quickly with an utterly cold-blooded smile. It was a giveaway. Cleary knew he was reacting to some knowledge about Nick's death. But what was it? Rosen either knew who had set up his brother, or he was the one behind it.

"See you around, Cleary."

"You can count on it."

FOURTEEN

Surprise Visit

The walls of his apartment seemed too close for comfort in the night heat. Cleary was frustrated. He felt he was closer to the truth about Nick's death, but the details still evaded him. He was circling the case, but not penetrating to the heart of it. He had circumstantial evidence in his hands, enough to toss Schneider and a few local DJs into jail, but probably not Rosen. And nobody was confessing to killing Williams or Nick.

He paced around the apartment, walked over to the wet bar. Nothing there. He had held off on buying a bottle, but now his resistance was weakening. He needed a drink.

Then he heard a whimper and saw the neglected black Lab puppy eyeing him from the kitchenette. It hobbled over to its empty dish with difficulty and nudged it, then looked up at Cleary. "*Jesus*. Just what I need. Reproach from a dog."

He walked over and picked up the pup. "Okay, you go out and do your business, and then you can eat." He carried the dog outside, then returned to the kitchenette. He reached into the cupboard for a can of dog food when something caught his eye. He hesitated a moment. Behind a box of Aunt Jemima pancake mix was a bottle of I.W. Harper he had overlooked the other night during his housecleaning.

He hastily opened the dog food, dished some into the bowl, then reached for the bottle of Harper and a clean glass. He stared at the bottle until his vision blurred. It was a moment of decision, a split in the road of his future. His thirst nagged like an itchy spot on his back he couldn't reach. But at the same time he knew one drink would lead to another, and by morning he would have lost the thread of his investigation. Nick's killer would slip away. Nick's killer, he thought, might even be counting on his drinking.

What the hell. He tilted the bottle toward him, opened it, then unceremoniously poured its contents down the drain. He turned on the faucet, washing away the alcohol smell, then filled the glass with water, and gulped it down. He picked up the dog's water bowl, refilled it, then walked over to the door. He opened it to call the pup.

For an instant, what he was seeing didn't register. Then he realized it was a pair of legs in nylons and high heels. He looked up to see Lana standing in the doorway, looking gorgeous and half-drunk, the pup in her arms.

"You know, it's rude to leave a party without saying good night, Detective."

For the second time this evening, the sight of her left him at a loss for words. "Would you like to come in?" he finally said.

"No, I'd like to stand on your doorstep all night holding a three-legged dog."

Cleary smiled. "Get in here." The scent of her perfume wafted about him like an aphrodisiac. He stepped aside, and she strolled into the room, setting the dog down, looking slowly around the apartment.

"What happened to your boyfriend?"

"He's not my boyfriend. He was a friend of Buddy's. He asked me to the party. I went." She smiled. "Never told him I was going home with him, though."

"Hope you didn't tell him you were coming here. I don't care for any more company tonight."

Lana smiled. "Neither do I."

"How about some coffee?" he asked.

"That sounds good. I sure don't need anything more to drink." She followed him into the kitchenette and leaned against the counter as Cleary got down the can of coffee. She nodded toward the empty bottle of Harper. "You don't look that drunk."

"Don't feel that drunk, either," he said, dropping the bottle in the trash. "'Cause I'm not."

He wished he had cleaned the place up a little, and felt obligated to apologize for the clutter. She laughed. "Don't worry about it, Jack. I probably shouldn't have just dropped by without an invitation."

"It's not like my social calendar's exactly crammed."

She opened the fridge and brought out the milk. She set it on the table and sat down, kicking off her heels. The pup, who'd just gobbled down the food Cleary had dished into his bowl, now hobbled over to Lana and plopped at her feet with a sigh. The coffee started to perk, and Cleary pulled out the chair across from her and sat. He brought out his pack of Luckys, offered her one, lit it for her. She sighed and dropped her head back, blowing smoke into the air. "So what'd you think of the party?"

"I coulda done without it."

She laughed. "Yeah, me too. But it passed the time. I seem to be doing a lot of that lately. Killing time."

Cleary realized he had neglected to get out mugs for their coffee and stood again and walked over to the cabinet. "Is this where you moved when you and your wife split?" she asked.

"It's cheap. It'll do for a while." He set the mugs on the counter, lifted the lid to the sugar bowl. It was empty. "Hope you take it without sugar."

"Fine. Whatever."

He poured the coffee, and picked up the cups. Just as he reached the table, he faltered as he saw he was about to step on the pup. Coffee sloshed over the side of the cup, onto his hands. He quickly placed the cups on the table and as he did more coffee spilled, this time splashing over Lana's leg.

"Oh, God, I'm sorry." He wiped his hands on his shirt, bent over, and helped her brush the coffee from her leg.

"It's okay, really," she said.

Then it happened suddenly, like the spilling of the coffee. Cleary's hand rested on Lana's leg, and she placed a hand over his. "What are we doing here, Jack?"

"I don't know," he said, then suddenly leaned toward her, his hand caressing the side of her face, his mouth moving closer and closer to hers. Their lips brushed. Hers were soft, and tasted faintly of booze and smoke. Her hand came up and rested lightly at the back of his neck. It felt cool against his skin. Now her mouth opened against his, and his arms came around her and he raised her to her feet, crushing her against him.

It had been so long since Cleary had held a woman, that a kind of fever gripped him as Lana pressed her body against his. She whispered his name. Her fingers slid through his hair. Jesus, but he wanted her. His mouth trailed down the side of her neck to her shoulder. He nudged the strap of her evening gown off her shoulder. Her skin smelled faintly of roses. His hands left her waist and slid upward along her ribs.

Then he stopped, withdrew his hands. He stepped back from her a little, pointed a finger at her. "I think we should drink our coffee," he said.

"Coffee? Oh. The coffee." Her glazed eyes danced with light.

He stared at her as she straightened her dress, composed herself. "Look, Jack, if you don't like me, why didn't you say something?" Her voice was slurred as she talked.

He walked over to the sink, turned on the faucet, and filled a glass with water. He drank half of it, his back to Lana, then turned to her. "I like you fine, Lana. It's just that..."

He watched as she sat down and sipped her coffee, her eyes lowered, her hair still mussed. Then she raised her gaze to meet his, and nodded. "I know. Some other time."

"Look, you take the bed and I'll bunk here on the couch, okay?"

She sniffled and looked up at him. Her mascara had smudged. Tears glistened on her cheeks. "I can't take your bed."

"Don't worry about it. Really. You need a shirt or something to sleep in?"

"Yes, thanks."

"Be right back."

He went into the bedroom, got a T-shirt out of the bureau, found an extra blanket and pillow in the closet, and returned to the living room. He dropped the bedding on the couch and passed Lana the T-shirt. "Here you go."

"Thanks," she said, and stood, clutching her evening dress against her. Then she rocked toward him, touching her mouth briefly to his. "You're a nice guy, Jack."

Yeah, he thought. He was so nice that he watched her pad down the hall, her beautiful ass swaying inside that dress, and wanted to hurry after her and rip it away, and make love to her long and hard.

Instead, he fixed up the couch, shucked his clothes, and stretched out. The pup hobbled over and Cleary reached down and brought him up onto the couch. The dog covered his face with wet, sloppy kisses. Wonderful. Is this my reward for not taking advantage of her?

Cleary lay awake a long time, his thoughts drifting back and forth between Lana and Ellen. He had once thought Ellen would be the only woman he would ever need in his life. She would fulfill his every need. Sure, he had thought about other women. What guy didn't? But, hell, he wasn't like some of the cops he knew who would screw a prostitute, then arrest her.

No, it wasn't infidelity that had caused their marriage to collapse. He had pushed her into it. Challenged her the same way he challenged the review board. And both times the results had been the same. You're out old pal, on your own. Fend for yourself.

Now Lana was a new start, filling the gap in his life. A new job, sure. He was working for her. But a new love? He could have had her so easily tonight. Yet he had stopped, because she was drunk and he was working for her. Simple as that. Except, it wasn't. He felt a deep compassion for her. She was like an expensive aged wine that was to be cherished until the right moment, rather than greedily gulped in a moment of selfish thirst. Maybe there would be a time for them. If he had anything to say about it, that time wasn't going to be too far in the future.

Lana opened her eyes, looked around in confusion, momentary panic. It was early morning and a shaft of sunlight was streaming into the bedroom window. Then she realized where she had spent the night, and slowly wiped away the cobwebs of sleep and recalled what had happened.

Oh, God. She felt embarrassed. She had to apologize to Cleary. At the same time she had a new admiration for him. Not many men would have taken her condition into consideration. She knew that from experience.

She sat up, stretched her arms. She was about to call Cleary's name, but decided against it. Instead, she climbed out of bed, and, still wearing Cleary's T-shirt, walked into the living room. She saw the pillow and rumpled blanket where he had spent the night. She stared at the couch, not yet comprehending that he wasn't in the apartment.

She walked into the kitchenette, and found a pitcher of orange juice resting on top of a note. She pulled it out, read it. Cleary apologized for leaving early, told her the coffee was ready, and to help herself to breakfast. He said he would call her at the beachhouse as soon as he knew something. She stood there reading the note a second and third time, thinking about Cleary's face. His mouth. She squeezed her eyes shut and hurried into the bedroom to get dressed.

She moved about Cleary's apartment, looking through his things. The more she could find out about him, the better off she would be. She lingered over pictures, one of Cleary and his estranged wife, another of Cleary and Nick together, both in uniforms.

She looked up over the picture to see the black Lab puppy staring at her. "Hi, cutie. Don't pay any attention to me, okay?"

The pooch whined.

She started opening a dresser drawer, glanced back again at the picture of the two brothers: the young, idealistic Cleary, and Nick beside him, grinning and proud. She pushed the dresser drawer closed.

She felt bad about what she was doing. She realized she was falling for him. It didn't make sense. It wasn't like her, but it was happening, and she couldn't bring herself to parade through his things.

Lana returned to the kitchen, where the pup whined as she approached. She patted the pooch on the head; he licked her hand. "Did he feed you, kid?" she asked.

The pooch whined again. She found an open can of dog food in the refrigerator, dished some into his bowl. "See you soon, Three Legs," she said softly, and left.

FIFTEEN

The Suspect

Cleary gazed out the second-floor window of a five-buck-a-night rattrap. It was a sparsely furnished single room where the air smelled faintly of mold and old socks, and you could hear the old guy upstairs taking a leak and coughing. But it had a view. The view was of a nondescript warehouse across the street, with an inconspicuous sign above the door that read: ROSEN ENTERPRISES. The early morning light spilled over the warehouse, washing it a dove gray, filling the row of windows just under the roof.

He hoped there would be a lot more to hear than there was to see. He placed a set of headphones over his ears, and began connecting a radio transmitter to a voice-activated Uher reel-to-reel tape recorder, which rested on a rickety desk next to him.

Cleary hadn't waited until Rosen's party to find out more about him. He had spent several hours yesterday watching Rosen's house, waiting patiently, which was an art itself. He had learned to deal with the boredom of surveillance in his years as a detective, and he could do a nine- or ten-hour stretch without getting antsy or fatigued. Finally, after five and a half hours, it had paid off. Rosen had left the house, and he had followed him here.

He knew his pursuit of Rosen as a suspect was largely based on a gut feeling that the man was linked to Nick's death. Now he had to find the hard evidence to prove it. Gut feelings were worthless in court, especially when the detective's emotions were spilling all over the place because the victim was his brother.

But there was no way for him to remain emotionally uninvolved in this case. Sure, nothing would bring back Nick, but he wouldn't be satisfied until he found his killers. In order of priorities, it ranked considerably higher than his floundering efforts to clear his own name.

The door opened, and Cleary turned to see Dottie breeze into the room. Her hair was disheveled and she looked beat, but she was carrying a take-out order of coffee and doughnuts, and a morning paper. She took one look around the room and wrinkled her nose. "Can't say much for the interior decorating," she remarked, closing the door.

He looked at the walls as if seeing them for the first time. "Guess I didn't take that into consideration."

"Remind me to get back to my pad in a couple hours. I'm expecting an eight A.M. wake-up call." She stabbed a thumb toward the window. "So what's the big deal with this Rosen guy, Jack? And it better be good, me gettin' up this early and all."

He hit a switch on the Uher; the tape recorder started to spin. "That's what I'm going to find out."

As Dottie set down his breakfast and paper, Cleary couldn't help but notice a couple of glaring hickeys on her neck, and Dottie didn't miss his scrutinizing look.

"Hey, stop the presses. So I had a date last night. What of it?"

"With what, a pit bull?"

She readjusted her collar and made a face that would fell timber as Cleary opened the paper. "You know a guy named Betts, Dottie?" he asked without looking up.

"Johnny Betts?" She reached for a doughnut. "'49 Merc, kind of a delinquent?"

"He was supposed to call me about something. I haven't heard from him." He was trying to ask her in a subtle way if Betts could be trusted.

She hesitated a moment, searching for the right words. "Nick said the kid comes from some pretty tough times. He's rough and kinda crazy, but according to your brother, he ain't short of heart."

Cleary nodded, filing it away for future reference, then, reacting to something in the paper, suddenly stood up. "Lock up for me, Dottie." He grabbed his coat and headed toward the door. "I've got some business downtown."

"Hey, what's the hurry, Cleary?"

"We'll talk later."

As he left, Dottie picked up the discarded paper, folded open to the tenth page. The top headline read: SUSPECT HELD FOR QUESTIONING IN RECORD PROMOTER MURDER.

Cleary arrived at the precinct house, mounted the familiar stairs he had climbed thousands of times over the years. Immediately a feeling of unease swept over him. He hadn't been here since the day he had been kicked off the force, suspended pending the review board hearing. From here, he had driven straight to the nearest joint that day and had drunk himself into a stupor. A couple of nights later, his marriage had ended. Nothing like cramming all your bad luck into seventy-two hours, he thought.

As he reached the top of the stairs and turned down the hall toward the detectives' offices, he remembered how proud he had been when he received his promotion to a plainclothes detective. There'd been some jealousy from the older guys, because he had climbed the ranks so fast. But no one ever said he didn't deserve it. They knew he had been determined, and had worked long and hard for it.

Nick was out of the service by then, and his agency was taking off. Jack wanted to help him out, but Nick insisted he never refer anyone from his own cases to him. It wouldn't look good for you, he had said. As it turned out, Nick didn't need his references. Right from the start, he had a knack for landing the big cases, the ones that paid Nick two or three times what he earned as a cop.

But that was all over.

He tried to shut off thoughts of the past as he entered the detectives' offices, and concentrate on the reason he was here. But his memories were like a leaky faucet that wouldn't stop dripping, and each drop seemed to explode in his head.

He found Fontana standing behind his desk in his cubbyhole office, staring out the window. More memories flashed through his mind: he and Fontana teaming up for the first time, working a fencing operation, and clicking together. The Wonder Boys, they had been called. Then Fontana turned about abruptly and looked stunned as he saw Cleary standing in the doorway.

"Jack, I didn't think I'd ever..." He shrugged. "...see you here again."

Cleary's eyes burned through him. "I read the paper this morning, Charlie. Thanks for keeping me informed. I sure appreciate it."

Fontana shoved his hands in his pockets, looked glumly at him. "Same to you, old partner. You didn't even tell me that Nick was keeping an eye on Williams. Had to find out second-hand from Dibble."

"Yeah. And did Dibble tell you that Nick was going up there expecting to hand over some tapes of Williams to you guys? Did he tell you that?"

Fontana's face, a face whose nuances Cleary had

once known so well, now became a mask, inscrutable. "How do you know that?"

"I've got my sources. Besides, you think Nick was the type who would sell out to the mob? You think both of us were crooked? Is that it? C'mon, Charlie. You can tell *me*. Is that what you think?"

"Jack, cut it out."

"Give me five minutes with Castellano, and I'll tell you if he was in on the hit."

"You know I can't do that." He rubbed his jaw. "Besides, he's been relased."

Cleary slammed his fist on the desktop, and glared at Fontana. "What? You kicked the bastard loose? What the hell is going on, Charlie?"

"Castellano was a *suspect*, Jack," he answered, a grim look on his face. "They released him after questioning."

"You said you'd keep me up to speed."

"This is *not* my case. Homicide's pissed off at me for leaning on 'em as much as I have. Now for your information I found out Castellano was cut loose fifteen minutes ago, and the next time you check with your secretary you'll find a message I called."

"Yeah, and the next time you see Donnie Castellano, it's gonna be in a canvas bag."

"I can't worry about that." Fontana's expression changed again, curious now. "What were you doing at that record party last night?"

Cleary gazed out the office window at the familiar faces in the squad room, and saw Dibble glance in his direction; Dibble with his pink Irish cheeks. He turned back to Fontana, wondering where he came into his information. "Maybe I was doing your work for you, Charlie."

"You mean you were screwing up my work," he shot back. "Damn it all, I've been working on that situation for the last six weeks, and I don't need you in there stirring up the friggin' bottom."

He stared at Fontana, a frown knitting on his brow. "Tell me what's going on. What investigation?"

"It's not for public consumption." He pointed a finger at Cleary. "You're just gonna have to trust me."

"I got a long way doing that on the city council case, didn't I?"

Cleary saw how the words struck Fontana like a fist, wounding him. There was a moment of silence as the invisible barrier between them took on form, shape, a label. Then Fontana marched across the room and slammed the door to his office. The sound reverberated through Cleary's bones.

"I did everything I could to keep you on the force. I took the stand, I vouched for you. I told 'em I thought the money was planted, that those mob boys set you up. They made it work. What in hell else was I supposed to do?"

Cleary looked at him glumly. "I don't know, Charlie. You tell me."

Fontana moved over to the window, hands in his pockets again as he gazed out. His shoulders were hunched, as if a Santa Ana was pushing at his back. "You know, I'm sick to hell of carrying this around with me. Everything's black and white to you."

Cleary said nothing.

Fontana looked over his shoulder. "So you got a

bad break. You still had friends in the department. With the right attitude you know damn well you could've gotten the review board to go easier."

He turned to face him. "'Stead of that you walked in there and spit in their eyes, came out and turned your back on everyone—you blew your marriage, shacked up with a bottle of bourbon and whoever else was alone at closing. I don't blame Ellen for what she did. What're you going to do if you're indicted, Jack? Piss on the jurors? That'll go over big."

"I can look at myself mornings, Charlie. Sounds to me like you're having problems in that department. I wouldn't doubt you set up that cowboy actor with Ellen. Is that it, you playin' matchmaker with your old partner's wife?" He laughed; it was a sharp, ugly sound that sliced through the air.

Some part of Cleary regretted the words as soon as they were out, but both had said too much for either to recant, and Fontana wasn't through yet. He spoke fast, his words aimed at Cleary's weak spots. And he knew just where to hit. That was how it was, Cleary thought dimly, when you worked the streets with a man. You learned where he was vulnerable, where he was strong.

"I've talked twice to Ellen since you broke up with her. Once at the funeral, and the other time after she kicked you out. I tried to talk her into taking you back. And believe me, doing something like that isn't easy for me."

He gazed at Cleary a moment. "She waited for you to come back and apologize, but you were too damn stubborn. She wasn't going to wait forever."

"Tough luck for me," Cleary snapped, stepping back. "At least I've still got my pride."

"Well, I hope your pride's enough for you, Jack. Maybe you can look at yourself mornings, but I'll tell you something. The other morning when I saw you, it wasn't very easy to look at you. That's a fact."

"If you can't tell by now, I'm through with the booze." His eyes met Fontana's. "I'm gonna find this guy, Castellano. I'm gonna get him."

S I X T E E N

Betts's Deal

The television in Johnny Betts's room at the Rocket Motel was tuned to an early morning Sunday show on which Horace Carter, a stony-faced, dark-suited brimstoner was railing at his audience.

". . . the obscenity and vulgarity of the rock and roll music is obviously a means by which the white men and his children can be driven to the level of the Negras. It is obviously Negra music. We considered it being the plot of the ideologists of the one-world race, the one-world economy, the one-world government. We used to call that the Communist ideology and I think we hit it on the head. . . ."

The phone rang in the corner, where Betts was lying on a sofa bed. He sat up groggily, stared at the phone resting next to his black leather jacket on the top of a disemboweled Mercury transmission. He stepped carefully across the floor, which was strewn with Carl Perkins albums, the remains of two six-packs, and a take-out pizza. He picked up the receiver on the third ring.

"Yeah?"

"Johnny."

"Rhonda. Watcha doin'?"

"Thinkin' about you."

"You naked or something?"

She let out a soft, coy laugh, and Betts's insides did a funny number. "Johnny, God, if my mother heard you say that. You should have heard her after you patched out last night. She thinks you're a bad influence."

"I am."

There was a pause as Johnny heard Rhonda telling her little brother to get out of the room. "That little brat gets worse every day."

"Did your ol' man find out we used his reel-to-reel?"

"Who cares? That stuff was so boring."

"It had its moments. If I got time, I'd like to find another recorder and use your ol' man's again to make copies for Cleary. You know anyone else with a reel-to-reel?"

"No."

"Neither do I."

"Johnny, you'd get in trouble if you made copies.

Those creeps play for keeps. . . . Benny! Get out!"

Betts waited until the shouting was finished, then said, "I hate to let Cleary down. Besides, I'll be long gone, and as soon as I get settled, I'll come get you, babe."

"Promise?"

"Definitely."

A soft giggle, then, "I'm ready to lay this city to rest. I'll be eighteen in twelve days. You won't forget me, will ya?"

"Hell no."

"Listen, I gotta get off the phone. This kid's drivin' me nuts. I'll call you right back as soon as I beat the crap out of him."

"Later."

Betts laid back in bed, stared at the ceiling. On the television, Carter was still ranting. ". . . is nothing more than an insidious tom-tom thumping designed to incite animalism, vulgarity, and sexual integration in our young . . ."

Betts walked over, stared at the screen a moment. "Up yours." He shut it off.

The phone rang again. "Hi, babe. Hope you didn't kill him."

There was silence at the other end of the line, then a deep, masculine voice. "Ready to move those tapes, kid?"

Betts rubbed his face. "You got ten thousand bucks to deal with me?"

He reached for a cigarette, lighting it from a pack of matches lying beside Cleary's lighter.

"We got ten thousand. We also got you made working for Jack Cleary, all right Johnny? You hear me?"

"I'm listening."

"I think we've met once before, Johnny. You remember?"

"Where would that be?"

"Up on Mulholland Drive. You called me a name, as I was talking with Nick Cleary."

"What of it? You killed him."

"Lemme tell you something. I know Nick was a friend of yours, but that's finished business, kid. You gotta ask yourself what's next on the agenda for Johnny Betts. Now you can play square with us on these tapes and get yourself a start in life, or you can dick around with his brother looking for payback and pocket money. If that's the way you're going, Johnny, save everybody a trip, all right? All you're gonna get is dead. Trust me on that one."

Betts stared at the metal suitcase beside the table. "Where and when?"

"The Hollywood sign. At noon."

"Let's make it tomorrow at noon."

"You got the tapes or not?"

"Ah—I got 'em."

"Noon, today."

"All right."

"You're doing the smart thing, kid."

Betts hung up the receiver and dropped the cigarette into a beer bottle. In a sudden burst of despair and self-revulsion, he picked up the phone, and threw it at the wall.

He pulled on his jacket, picked up the suitcase of

tapes, put the receiver back on the phone, and walked out, slamming the door.

In the parking lot of the motor court, he blinked at the bright sun, perched against the blue of the sky like a huge yellow grapefruit. Then he strode over to the Mercury, which was parked next to a couple of full-dress Harleys and a Chevy step-side. The latter was new in the lot, and normally he would've looked it over. Not today.

Even the new paint job on the Merc didn't catch his eye as he unlocked the door, slipped behind the wheel, and laid the suitcase on the other front seat. He lit a cigarette, staring straight ahead as he smoked. Then he gunned the engine, backed up, and screeched out, leaving a twenty-foot patch.

Cleary stopped at a pay phone outside police headquarters, and dialed. "KGFJ, can I help you?" a woman answered.

"Hi, there. I'm wondering if the Gator is doing his show today."

"Eleven to three, every Sunday. Monday through Thursday, he's—"

"Thanks," Cleary said, and hung up. He quickly dialed the number Baytor had given him. He told him what he needed, listened to the expected argument, then laid out the threat again, promising to personally deliver the ledger sheet to the DA. "All right, Cleary. Meet me at ten-thirty in the parking lot of the station."

"I thought you'd see it my way."

"Just be there on time, or you'll miss me. I got a show to do."

Cleary pressed the button disconnecting the call, dropped another nickel in the phone, and made another call. This one promised to be more pleasing.

"Lana."

"Hi, Jack."

He imagined her lying on the terrace of the beachhouse, sunning herself, gorgeous in her one-piece swimsuit. He thought momentarily of what had happened—and not happened—and felt a quick tightening in his gut. "Just wanted to make sure you lived through my coffee."

"Never felt better. Thanks for being so nice last night, Jack."

"Let's try it again sometime."

"I think I'd like that."

"Listen, I may have a line on one of the guys the police have been questioning about your husband's death." He glanced at his watch.

"Oh?"

"If you're home later, I'll call and let you know what I turned up."

"I'll be home. Jack, be careful."

Cleary's insides stirred at the soft, sensual tone of her voice. He was surprised by how long it had been since he had felt so warmed by a disembodied voice. The taste of her skin suddenly seemed to fill his mouth. He could barely spit out an "Okay."

He hung up, his hand lingering on the receiver, as though it connected him somehow to Lana. *Later*, he told himself. *Later there'll be time for Lana.* Then he dug into his pocket for another nickel.

He dialed again—Betts's number this time. The phone rang, continued ringing. Cleary replaced the receiver, glanced at his watch again, and hurried away.

At the instant the phone was ringing in Betts's motel room, he was looking up to the Hollywood sign stretching across the hill in the distance. He was about to collect an easy ten grand. Freedom money. Enough money to blow this town for good. To start over. Once he picked up the dough, all he had to do was swing by the motel, clean house, and he would be gone. Good-bye L.A.

Despite the sweet seduction of the fantasy, Betts didn't feel too good about it. In fact, he felt pretty damn bad about it, as if buried inside the fantasy was a dark and spreading doom that was going to leap out at him and smother him once he accepted the money.

But hey, a guy had to look out for himself, didn't he? Wasn't that the way it worked?

Cleary beat Bobby Baytor to the KGFJ parking lot by five minutes. The Gator, decked out in a lime-green Don Loper suit, drove up in his '55 white-with-coral-and-black Packard Caribbean convertible. The cool, smooth upsweep of the chrome vines on his car was a total contrast to the Gator's manner as Cleary came around to his door.

"I don't suppose you give a rat's ass that meeting me here is taking a hell of a chance."

"I'm your cousin, remember?"

"Not everyone's gonna fall for that. You're getting pretty well known lately."

"That come with a volume control, Gator?" he said, gesturing toward Baytor's suit.

"Your problem, Cleary, is that you got no class. You know that?"

"And I'm supposed to take lessons from you? Yeah. Sure. So where's Castellano?"

Baytor gave him a disgusted look, then handed him a slip of paper. "Finito, Cleary—no more names, no more addresses, no more telephone numbers. And if you want some good advice I'd take that ten grand and blow town. Your ass has been parked overtime in this town for a week now."

"What ten grand? What are you talking about?"

Baytor stepped out of his car. "I just heard some-one's collecting on those tapes today for ten large ones. I figured it was you."

"Well, figure again."

S E V E N T E E N

Hot Tub
Interrogation

The motel was a sorry-looking dump that reminded him of a beached whale in the hot light. Cleary drove by it once and pulled into the alley behind it. He noticed the windows looking out on the lot, and drove on. He parked the Eldorado halfway down the next block, close to a wall, where it was out of sight. He checked his .45, made sure he had extra ammo, then got out and closed the door softly.

Heat radiated from the black asphalt, soaking his shirt in seconds as he walked back to the building. He barely noticed the heat. His jaw was set with grim determination as he moved around the side of the building toward the front. Toward Donnie Castellano's room.

There were cars in the front lot, their hoods gleaming with sunlight, but no one was around. It was like everyone had fled, leaving behind their wheels, clothes, their belongings. Cleary found Room 10 at the end of the hall. The door was closed, but a suitcase rested in the hallway just outside it. It looked like Castellano was leaving in a big hurry.

Cleary quietly moved the suitcase aside. He flattened his back against the wall, touched the knob of the door lightly, testing to see if it was locked.

It wasn't.

He smiled. Careless, very careless, Castellano, he thought. He turned the knob slowly until it was unlatched, and pushed it open an inch or so.

He gripped his .45 in both hands, swallowed hard, and then leaped forward and delivered a swift, powerful kick to the door. It burst open, startling Castellano, who was packing his bags. He spun around from the shelf he was emptying, and reached under his arm for his piece. But Cleary was already on him. The butt of the gun smashed into Castellano's jaw, and he crumpled to the floor.

It was one of the most satisfying acts of Cleary's life.

Before Castellano could recover, Cleary disarmed him, ripped an electrical cord out of the lamp, and tied his feet together. He cuffed his hands behind his back and began dragging him toward the bathroom. Just as he pulled him to the doorway, Castellano came awake and struggled to sit up.

"What the hell are you doing? Just who the…"

"Watch your language," Cleary said, and stuffed one of Castellano's rolled-up socks into the man's mouth. He stepped into the bathroom, turned on the hot water. It drummed into the tub as Cleary grabbed Castellano by the feet, and lugged him into the bathroom.

Cleary lit a cigarette, flipped down the lid of the toilet and sat on it, watching Castellano sprawled next to the tub. Castellano grunted. He bucked. He tried to free his bound feet. His face turned lobster red.

"I'm gonna make it real simple for you," Cleary said, leaning toward him. "Who hired you for the hit on Mulholland Drive?"

Castellano shouted into the sock; it sounded like he had a mouthful of marbles.

"Care to repeat that?" Cleary asked, and jerked the sock from his mouth.

Castellano sucked at the air, then snapped his head to the left, toward the steam billowing from the tub. He looked back at Cleary. "I'll make it simple for *you*. You got no shot: whatever you could do is not half what they'd do to me if I told you."

"I'm glad we both want to keep this nice and simple." Cleary flicked his butt into the tub and, without another word, hoisted Castellano like a bag of potatoes and dumped him into the tub.

Castellano winced as the steaming water soaked through his clothes and began searing his flesh. Still, he seemed capable of bearing the pain. "Save us both some time, pal. I've got five grand in my suitcase.

Take that and split, 'cause I'm not gonna tell you."

Cleary ignored him. He reached up to a shelf over the sink and plugged in a radio. Castellano's eyes widened with astonishment—and then fear—as he realized that the steaming water was just the beginning. Cleary balanced the radio on the flat rim of the tub and slowly nudged it toward the edge, his smile growing as he did so, his eyes now a polished sheen.

"Simple, right?" Cleary said. "We want to keep it simple. So I'm gonna ask you once more. Who hired you for the hit on Mulholland?"

"Aw, hey, wait a second," Castellano said. "Just hold on there."

Cleary leaned over, turned off the water. "I didn't hear you, Donnie. Who hired you?" Cleary asked in the same calm voice, a voice that whispered with death. He saw panic coiled in Castellano's eyes. The radio wobbled on the edge of the tub.

"Hey, man. What are you? Warped?" Castellano shouted. "Now c'mon, man, you can't do this."

"That was my brother up there on Mulholland, Donnie boy."

"Okay. Eddie Rosen. Rosen hired me!" Castellano yelled, his eyes fixed on the radio, his bound feet kicking.

The radio began a slow dip toward the water. Castellano's eyes bulged with terror. Then Cleary jerked the cord just as the radio slipped over the edge. It dangled just inches above the water. "I wouldn't kick so much if I were you."

"Oh, God, oh, God, I'm gonna have a heart attack. Get that thing away."

"Tell me everything you know."

Castellano's head jerked past Cleary toward the door.

"I'll be very interested in hearing that myself," Dan Dibble said as he entered the bathroom.

"This guy was about to blow town." Cleary was still holding the radio just above the surface of the water.

Dibble's smile was friendly. "You're two steps ahead of me as usual, Jack." He turned his eyes on Castellano. "Got yourself into a hell of a fix there, didn't you?" He looked back at Cleary. "Interesting interrogation technique. I must've missed it in the manual."

"Eddie Rosen put the hit on my brother," Cleary said. "You heard this scumbag. You heard it, Dan. You're the witness."

Dibble nodded.

"You know who Rosen is, Dan?"

Dibble smiled. "Sure. He hasn't exactly escaped my attention." He pointed to the .45 exposed in Cleary's shoulder holster. "Let me have the piece, Jack."

Cleary hesitated, looked from Castellano to Dibble.

"Jack, it's not like I'm talking to a civilian." He sounded annoyed. "Lemme do my job, will ya?"

Dibble stuck out his hand. Finally Cleary pulled out the .45. He hesitated again. "I want everything out of this guy, Dan."

"Don't worry. I'm gonna handle him for you. Just watch."

Cleary reluctantly handed the .45, butt end first, to Dibble.

"There we go. Now the other one." He nodded toward the bulge in the back of Cleary's coat. "Just toss it through the door out of our way."

"That's my gun," Castellano shouted as Cleary pulled the .38 from the back of his belt.

"Shut up," Dibble growled. "You don't need it any more."

Then, matter-of-factly, he trained Cleary's gun on Castellano, who, panicking, tried to stand up. Dibble pulled the trigger, and blew him into the wall. Castellano, in the split second of life that remained in him, looked down in horror at the blood seeping from his chest, across the front of his shirt. His eyes widened, his mouth yawned open in a silent scream, and he slid down the wall, trailing blood, which bubbled pink in the water around him.

"What the hell are you doing?" Cleary yelled.

"What the hell does it look like?" There was a defiant, belligerent edge to Dibble's voice that made Cleary acutely uneasy.

"This is getting to be a habit between you and me, Jack. You know that?"

Suddenly Cleary understood. He understood, and almost wished that he didn't. Damn it, no. "You. For chrissakes, Dan. It was you, wasn't it? You set me up on that bribery rap. You lousy bastard."

"You never get the message, do you, Cleary?" Dibble shook his head. "You're one of those pains in the ass, you know that, Cleary? One of those guys who doesn't want to turn a buck, but doesn't want to mind his own business, either. That's a real dangerous way to be, Cleary."

A tight smile turned on Cleary's lips. "I had a feeling someone inside the department was involved. What were you doing? Providing protection for one of our esteemed city councilmen? Sure, I know that game. Our good lawmaker uses a dirty badge to keep the cops out of his hair so he can reap the unofficial rewards of public office, thanks to the donations of the mob. That's how it goes, doesn't it, Dibble? C'mon, you can tell me. It wouldn't make much difference now."

"Big hot-shot crusader. You were warned off that city council corruption thing three different times." His mouth twisted into a sneer. "It's guys like you, Cleary, who screw everything up."

"You stink, Dibble. I'm gonna get you. You're gonna go down for this."

Dibble laughed. "You think so?"

Cleary cocked his head as he heard the shriek of approaching sirens.

"Yeah, you're dealing nothing but aces, Cleary. My uniforms are gonna be through that door in about thirty seconds. I'm gonna tell 'em you shot the guy just before I got here, then you turned the piece on me and I had to blow you away." He grinned, pulling out his own gun, dropping Cleary's in the tub.

"Oh, oh. There go the prints." Dibble smiled. "You're big on investigations, Cleary. Don't you think that'll play in Peoria?"

Since the moment Dibble shot Castellano, Cleary had been aware his number was up, too. But he had one hope. Castellano's body, perched on the edge of the tub, had been slowly slumping to one side. All of his quiet-voiced posturing had been an effort to delay Dibble, in the hopes of breaking his concentration for one moment. That was all he could hope for, but it might be all he needed.

Suddenly Castellano's body fell, and Dibble turned his head. In that instant Cleary lunged at him, knocking his gun hand in the air. Dibble slipped on the wet floor, fell, and cracked his head on the edge of the tub.

The gun slipped from his hand. Cleary scooped it up as he heard the footfalls of the officers entering the house. There was only one escape route and, the way his luck was running, he might not even make it out alive. He crossed his arms in front of his face and hurtled himself head first through the window. Glass exploded around him, and for a split second the world was only the sound of the shattering glass, and the heat. Then he landed on his hands and knees, rolled, scrambled to his feet.

"You dirty son of a bitch, Dibble," he hissed, but didn't look back. He raced down the alley to the Eldorado, adrenaline pumping through him like there was no tomorrow.

E I G H T E E N

The Fugitive

Cleary drove aimlessly for an hour, torn by indecision. He had escaped injury in his desperate getaway, but he didn't have the foggiest notion what to do next. It seemed as if his mind had split down the middle, and the two parts were battling each other for dominion.

One part of him said to call Fontana, his old partner, a man he had trusted for years. But the other part said Fontana was a cop, that Fontana wasn't going to endanger himself. The man had a wife, kids to think about. What good would it do to tell him Dibble was dirty, that Dibble had shot Castellano? What would Fontana do, arrest Dibble because his ex-partner who'd been kicked off the force said so? It wouldn't happen. It was that simple.

But nothing else was simple.

Why did Dibble want Castellano dead? It had to mean he was somehow connected with the Williams case. But how?

Think it through. You'll find the answer if you think it through.

He pulled onto a side street and parked. He lit a Lucky. He sat back. Closed his eyes. There. Better. Now he could think. The warm late afternoon air slid into the car, smoother than smoke. All right. Where did it start?

Dibble had been a friend of his brother's. Not a close friend, but still a friend. Nick was so involved in his cases, he probably was unaware of Dibble's after-hours activities. Yet, he might turn to the detective for help. Suppose Nick had called Dibble after the Williams hit and told him about the tapes? He wanted to unload them, and rack up some PR with the department at the same time.

But Dibble had sold him out. Dibble had gone to Rosen, who'd sent his own team to pick up the tapes. Rosen had ordered Williams's hit, then Nick's.

He blew smoke at the windshield; his eyes were glassy, distant. That wasn't all. If Dibble worked for Rosen, then Rosen was probably the mobster behind the payoffs to the city councilmen. It was all coming together. It was Rosen's plan to set up the bribery rap against him. A direct hit would have been too obvious, would have sent waves across the state that the mob was killing cops. He had too good a deal going to jeopardize it.

Instead, he had used slow torture. First, the job; then...Ellen. Had Ellen already met her cowboy before their marriage fell apart? He wondered now if it was an accident that she had met him. Maybe she had been duped, willingly so, but still duped. Rosen had been counting on him to kill himself with booze.

He realized he wasn't far from the Rosen Enterprises office. He started the engine. He would go back up to the hotel room. He didn't care about the tapes anymore. He knew where Rosen stood. But there was something else he had left in the room that he was going to need.

First he had to get to Fontana. Someone had to be told. He drove around the corner, spotted a phone booth, checked to make sure there were no cops around. Then he parked and got out. He dialed the precinct number.

"Charlie, it's Jack. Have you heard any—"

"For chrissake, Cleary. What the hell happened in that motel room?"

"I haven't got time to get into it, but believe me you're not getting the right story."

"Well, they're about to put half the force on picking you up."

"Charlie, Dibble's up to his neck in this shit. He's a front for—"

"Listen, I can't talk now."

"I want to see you."

"Look. I'm a cop, Jack." His voice was almost a

whisper. "If I see you, I'll have to bring you in. You know that."

"Charlie, for God's sakes, didn't you hear what I said?"

Cleary listened to Fontana exhale into the phone. He knew he was asking him to cross a line, to chance the same fate that he had met. "I've got some business I have to take care of. I'll meet you in two hours at the pier."

"Thanks, Charlie."

A few minutes later, Cleary drove past Rosen Enterprises, parked in a space behind the hotel, and climbed the back stairway to the room. He was absorbed in his own thoughts and wasn't really aware of anything else until he opened the door of the room. Then he froze at the sight in front of him.

Seated by the window next to the reel-to-reel, wearing the headphones, was Johnny Betts. He took them off and held up a hand when he saw Cleary. "That steno of yours said I might find you here. Heard you've been looking for me."

Cleary stared at him without answering. He closed the door, leaned back against it, crossed his arms. "Figured you'd be either dead or on your way out of town by now."

Betts lowered his eyes to the floor. "You said before you like to know who you're working with. Well, as anyone back home'd be happy to tell you, I'm the son of a roadhouse tramp who split when I was ten and a daddy that..." He shrugged, a slight smile curled on his mouth. "He's your standard redneck badass. Years that he wasn't in jail he'd come home three nights a week and beat the livin' crap out of me for lookin' like him."

He shifted in the chair, glanced briefly at the slowly turning reel-to-reel. "Time since I was twelve I was in foster homes and correctional institutions. Broke parole from an auto theft to come out here last year. Guess the apple don't fall too far from the tree. Hell, if it wasn't for your brother, I'd still be doing the same damn thing."

"I heard on the street someone was selling the tapes," Cleary said.

"You heard right."

"Did you get your price?"

Betts met Cleary's gaze for the first time, then he reached under the chair. From between his legs, he pulled out the metal valise. "I told myself I'd take the ten grand and get a fresh start. 'Bout three-quarters of the way up Mulholland I figured I'd had my quota of those."

"You didn't sell them?"

Betts pushed the suitcase toward Cleary with his foot. "They're all in there. Enough to put Rosen away for Buddy Williams, bribing cops and politicians, bootlegging records through Starlite, selling 'em off the books, and about forty other things."

Cleary rolled forward on the balls of his feet and opened the suitcase. Jesus. They were here. All of them right here. He let his fingers slide across them, as if confirming their reality, then looked up at Betts.

"I don't know about the folks back home, Betts, but from where I'm standing you look like a pretty solid guy."

From the look in Betts's eyes, it was obvious what Cleary had said meant a lot to him.

Cleary walked over to a closet, pulled out a suitcase, and began filling it with weapons he had stashed in the back of the closet. There were several handguns, a submachine gun, a sawed-off shotgun, and enough ammo to hold off a serious siege.

"Hey, what's going on?" Betts asked.

"Lot of heat's coming down. All on me."

Cleary handed Betts the suitcase of weaponry, then grabbed the other one. "I'm taking the tapes. You hold onto the hardware. If I haven't called your place in twenty-four hours get out of town."

"What's happening? C'mon, I wanna know. I wanna help you."

"I'm going to deliver these tapes for Nick. They're going to finally get in the right hands. Be around if I make the call. Now get out of here."

Betts opened the door, started to leave, then stopped and looked back. "Hey, Cleary." He tossed him a nickel, which Cleary snared.

"What's this for?"

"I wanna hear from you."

A brief look passed between them, then Betts was out the door. Cleary, closing up shop, was about to turn off the Uher and the radio receiver when he glanced out the window. His features suddenly tightened as he spotted a familiar black '55 Ford parked in the alley beside Rosen's building.

He reached over and turned up the volume on the recorder. "... do business in Hollywood, Rosen, you need me. I can either keep you open or shut you down. But the money for my guys goes directly to me, and I'll tell you when and where. What do you say?"

Cleary felt the shift inside his chest, as if his heart were sliding from one side to the other. He shut his eyes. Rubbed them. Oh God. It was the last person he wanted to hear. He knew that voice. It was achingly familiar. It was the same voice he had heard on the phone half an hour ago.

"If everything checks out like you say, Fontana, we'll be in touch."

Cleary heard footsteps receding, a door closing, and after a moment, another voice. "What do we need him for, Eddie? We've already got a detective in our pocket."

"You can never have enough of them. Believe me, cops and politicians are the cheapest dollar you spend."

Cleary peered out the window as the door to Rosen's office opened, and Fontana walked out. The man he thought he could trust glanced around once, then headed for the Ford. He gazed at the back of his former partner's head, willing him to look around, to look around and up. *Hey, Charlie ole boy. Up here. It's me. Your ole pal, Jack.*

But Fontana kept moving, and a sickening feeling spread out across the floor of Cleary's gut.

He wanted to puke.

Streaks of rose and lavender slid across a sky the color of plums, and curved down, striking the waters off the Santa Monica pier. Fontana consulted his watch, then glanced out toward the water where a gull in mindless grace soared skyward. He dropped his cigarette, crushed it under his heel. He glanced down the street for a long moment, as if he were expecting company, then looked at his watch again. He climbed into his car and drove away.

As the car vanished in the distance, Cleary stepped out from the side of a building where he had been watching Fontana. He gazed out as the last sunlight failed, and the sky turned a deep, hopeless violet.

N I N E T E E N

Night Visit

The Eldorado whispered through the streets as Cleary sought a steadiness of spirit, a resolve not to capitulate to the odds stacking up against him like a bad hand in poker. He knew it might not be enough to save him, but without it he was surely lost. Already, the night seemed to be conspiring against him. The harsh, neon-lit streets looked mean, the dark buildings indifferent. Furtive figures slipped through the shadows, any of whom could be looking for him, setting traps, ready to open fire.

You are in deep trouble, buddy.

He tried to blank his mind of his fears, yet they

haunted him. He would die alone, the victim of a mob hit, or worse, by the hand of his old friends and fellow detectives. He imagined Dibble holding a gun to his head, and Fontana red with laughter as he shouted, *You fool. You can't trust anyone. When are you going to learn that?* And then he saw Ellen, her arms wrapped around the cowboy actor, as she shook her head and denied knowing him.

A cop car pulled alongside him in the next lane. Cleary stifled an impulse to slam his foot against the accelerator and flee for his life. Was the guy watching him? Did he recognize him? Was he about to pull a gun? *Oh Christ*, he pleaded silently with the cop inside. *Just keep on moving, buddy. I'm no one you want.*

He turned at the corner, smoothly, easily, then turned again in an alley, and slowed. Sweat pimpled his forehead, his temples. He felt like he used to after a bender—the inside of his mouth tasted raw and thick, his hands trembled, a knot the size of a golf ball tightened in his gut.

He glanced in the rearview mirror. The alley was as dark and empty as a waiting tomb. *Calm down, man. You gotta be able to think straight.* On the street again, he scanned the cars. No cops. For the moment, he was anonymous, safe.

He drove on, paying little attention to where he was. At some point, he crossed a familiar route and, without thinking about it, swung into a turn and followed it. He didn't realize he was headed back for another glimpse of his past until he was just blocks from the house. His old place. The knot that had settled in his gut now leaped into his chest. He drove slowly past the house. The lights were on. He wondered what Ellen was doing. Cooking? Eating? Talking on the phone? *Entertaining the cowboy actor?*

He came around the block, stopped in front. It was foolish to be here. It was such an obvious place to look for him. But he didn't care. He shoved the car into gear when he saw Ellen strolling under a streetlamp, her hair drawn away from her face with a kerchief. She was carrying a bag of groceries from the corner market, and when she saw the Eldorado she stopped, staring in disbelief. Then she looked around nervously and hurried over to the car, opening the passenger door.

"Jack, what're you doing here? They're saying on the news that you killed a man. What's going on?"

A pulse beat at his temple as his hand slid inside his jacket and brought out his gun. He pointed it at her. "Get in the car."

Her dark eyes widened in terror. "Jack, what's happened to you?"

"Get in. Now." He spoke calmly, slowly. But his teeth were clenched. He literally saw red. *Control yourself, Cleary.* "I'm not going to hurt you, Ellen. Just get in."

She slid inside, and he stepped on the gas before she had closed the door. It slammed shut as he took off down the road. "Jack," she hissed. "Have you lost your mind? Where're you taking me?"

"For a ride, Ellen. Put the bag down on the floor. I've got a few questions."

"So do I," she said, and set the groceries down between her feet. "What makes you think you can kill someone just because you think he might have killed Nick? You've really gone off the deep end this time. And I'm really not surprised, you know that? I'm not one goddamn bit surprised because this is how you used to get when you were drunk. Only now you're sober, so you can't even blame it on booze."

"I didn't kill him." He put the gun back in his shoulder holster. "Remember that big, friendly, Irish detective, Dan Dibble?"

When she didn't answer, he continued. "Dan killed him. You want to know why?"

She whipped the kerchief off her head and shook her hair free. "What's this got to do with me?"

He laughed. "Dibble, Ellen, is working for the man who killed Nick. A guy named Eddie Rosen."

He glanced at her. Her eyes were wide with terror. She looked as if she was ready to leap from the car.

"We're going to just keep driving around tonight, Ellen, until you've told me what I want to know."

"Are you going to torture me like you did to that man in the motel if I don't answer?"

"No," he said softly.

She sensed she had the upper hand. "Take me home right now, Jack. Then, if I were you, I'd get out of town fast."

"Like I said, you're not going anywhere until I get some answers. I won't hurt you, but someone else might. Cops see this car, who knows what might happen."

She shifted in her seat. "Jack, please, you're just going to make it rougher on yourself if—"

"I imagine Rosen's guys are looking for me, too. Wouldn't that be a sweet end? Machine-gunned down together, Mr. and Mrs. Cleary."

"All right, Jack. What's your question? Am I seeing Tex Harris? Yes. Do I love him? None of your business. It happens that he's good to me, very good, and I like that. Maybe I love him for it. So what?"

"I want to know how you met him, when and where. Tell me that."

She made a soft, almost inaudible sound, perhaps a sigh of sudden understanding. "Okay, I get it. You want to know if I was seeing him when we were together, right? Is that it? Well, it so happens that I did meet him before we separated, but nothing happened until after we split up."

"Where'd you meet him?"

"At a department store while I was shopping." She was looking down now as she talked, smoothing her hands over her skirt. "He complimented me on a blouse I tried on, then before I knew it, he paid for it. I told him I was married and couldn't accept it, but he said he had plenty of money and it was okay."

Yeah, swell, Cleary thought. He could just imagine some big, raw-boned cowboy, spewing out a string of "shucks" and "ma'ams," and pulling out a wad of bills.

"When did that happen?"

"Oh, about a week before you were suspended. He wanted to see me again, but I told him I couldn't. Then a few days later... after we ended it, I ran into him again."

"Where?"

"At a party. I was feeling crummy, and got invited to a party, okay? He was there."

"Whose party?"

"I don't know. It doesn't matter."

She was lying. He could detect a slight quaver in her voice. "Whose party was it, Ellen?" His voice held a cold, manic edge, and she heard it.

"Someone in the movie business."

He looked over at her, still doubtful that she was telling the truth. "Who invited you?"

She was staring out the window. "Where're we going, Jack? Take me home. Please." She reached out, touched his leg. "You said you'd take me home."

He brushed her hand away; her fingers curled in on themselves.

"We're not through yet, Ellen."

"We *are* through, you bastard," she spat. "Get that straight, Jack. You and I are done. Over. The divorce is just a formality. Now turn around, damn it. I mean it, Jack. Turn this car around."

"I meant you're not through answering me. I know where you and I stand." If anything, the gap between them was so wide now, that it couldn't have been bridged even if he had wanted it to be. The curious part was that he no longer felt anything for her. Nothing except resentment, anger, and the incipience of hatred that would turn dark and dangerous if he discovered she knew more than she was letting on.

Please, Ellen, don't know any more.

"Who invited you to the party?" he repeated.

She sighed and ran her hands over her face. "All

right. It was Helen, Helen Dibble. She felt sorry for me. She knew what I was going through."

"And your cowboy just happened to be there?"

"Yes. Is that so strange? Actors have been known to party with other movie people."

"What about the Dibbles? It doesn't exactly sound like their kind of crowd. I mean I've never known Dibble to hang around with movie people."

"Dan said he does some after-hours security work for the guy who was putting on the party. That's all I know."

Cleary wondered if Ellen was substituting movie for record industry people, and the party was actually put on by someone like Mickey Schneider.

"Let me tell you about someone else that Dibble happens to work for, namely Eddie Rosen."

"I don't want to hear it, Jack. It doesn't involve me."

"I think it does, because I think Dibble set you up." He pulled into an alley, shifted into neutral, and held his foot against the brake. As the car idled, and the moon traveled in its solitary journey across the dark, unforgiving L.A. sky, he told her everything he knew.

She listened with her head bowed, then when he was finished, sat quietly a moment, digesting it all. He wasn't sure what he expected: disbelief, remorse, possibly anger at being duped. But the moment she opened her mouth, he knew it wasn't going to be any of those things.

"Jack, I'm sorry about what happened to you and Nick. I really am. But that's over. Nothing will bring Nick back. And I know you were warned about that city council investigation. You told me yourself. You should have dropped it."

"Dropped it because someone told me to?"

"For your own safety."

"Wake up, Ellen. You think your cowboy is going to give a damn about you when this is over? You were used by Dibble. He was trying to destroy me for nosing into the mob. Your cowboy was just playing another role."

She shook her head vehemently. "You're wrong. Well, maybe what you say was true at first. But Tex cares for me. I know he does. He asked me to marry him, and I accepted."

"*Marry* him?" Cleary nearly choked on the word.

"When our divorce is final."

Marry. That's what she's saying, man. M-A-R-R-Y.

Cleary slammed the Eldorado into gear and pulled out of the alley. He drove in silence, remembering again Nick's prophetic statement about Ellen. He felt numb, cold, despite the heat. He braked at a red light, leaned across Ellen, opened the door. "Get out, and take your groceries."

She looked around frantically. "I don't know where I am. You can't leave me here. You said you'd take me home. How can I carry this bag of groceries home? Jack? Jack, listen to me."

He reached into his pocket, pulled out the nickel Betts had given him earlier. "Call Tex, and tell *him* to take you home."

T W E N T Y

The Refuge

Cleary knew he couldn't go home, and he knew he couldn't drive around all night. The later the hour became, the greater the chances a police cruiser would pull him over. The tapes were locked in the trunk with plenty of evidence to support his story. Yet, he seriously doubted that either he or the evidence would see the dawn if he turned himself in. He could imagine the headlines in tomorrow's papers: FORMER COP DIES IN SHOOT-OUT, or, KILLER-COP TAKES OWN LIFE. At best, FORMER DETECTIVE CHARGED IN MURDER RAP.

He was heading in the direction of the beach,

pulled toward the one person who seemed to care that he was alive. He arrived at the beachhouse unannounced. There was a light on inside when he knocked. He waited, knocked again. Finally he heard a voice. "Who is it?"

"Lana, it's me. Jack."

The door opened slowly. Lana wore a white silk robe and was silhouetted against the illumination behind her. A nimbus of light surrounded her head like a halo, so that she seemed angelic, not quite real. But when she reached for his hand and drew him into the house, he knew she was not only real, but that she was his harbor.

"You surprised me," she said, shutting the door behind them.

"Sorry, I should've called before—"

"No, I'm glad you came. I wanted to see you. I've been calling all night. God, you look—is something wrong, Jack? What happened?"

He stepped inside, noticed the glass door was open to the deck. He stiffened, suspecting someone else was here—Dibble or Rosen's thugs. He glanced at Lana, who gave him a puzzled look.

He crossed the living room, stepped through the doorway and onto the wide deck facing the ocean, looked about. It was empty, except for the deck chairs and table where they'd eaten lunch that day lifetimes ago.

He drank in the warm ocean air, tried to relax. "What is it, Jack?"

He turned to her. "You didn't hear anything on the radio about what happened?"

"I haven't listened to it all day. For God's sakes, Jack, tell me what's—"

"Can we sit down?"

"Let me get you a drink."

"Water's fine," he said, easing himself into one of the chairs at the deck table.

When she returned with his water, she suggested they sit on the lounge chairs, which were more comfortable. A full moon, tinged a bloody red, was rising. Waves crashed down on the shore, shattering the glistening moonbeams, as Cleary told her about his day. At one point, his ennui became so great, he stood, paced along the deck, and finally stopped at the railing, gazing out at the sea.

"I used to feel at home in the world, surrounded by things I could believe in." His voice was steady, emotionless. "Now, I don't know what to believe in anymore. The last couple of months I've cut myself off from anything or anyone who could make me feel the way I used to."

Lana walked over, stood next to him. "Jack," she interrupted. "There's something I need to tell you. I—"

Anticipating her, he took a step closer to her, placed a hand on her shoulder. "Me first." His hand slid around her. He embraced her.

"Jack, please. I—"

Then Cleary kissed her, and her body seemed to melt into his, and he knew this would be no repeat of last night. Their desire for each other was mutual. Without speaking, they went inside.

In the doorway of the bedroom, he pulled her

gently against him, kissing her, and her hunger became a low, feverish moan as her mouth opened
against his. It tasted faintly of Scotch. His hands slid
down the curve of her spine, then around to the sash
at her waist. He untied it. The silky folds of her robe
fell open and his hands slid inside, against skin softer
than a baby's, over the flare of her hips, up to her
breasts, reading her contours and curves and planes
like a blind man.

His fingers dipped inside the waistband of her
panties, then drew them off as she lifted one foot,
then the other, kicking them away, her mouth never
leaving his, her hands working at the zipper on his
slacks, the buttons on his shirt. He didn't know how
long they stood there in the doorway, caressing each
other, murmuring softly, their words lost in the haze
of desire, but at some point, he simply picked her up
and carried her over to the bed.

The mattress sank with their weight. She reached
out with her arms and he slipped into them as if he
had been doing it all his life. In the moonlight that
seeped through an opening in the curtain, her skin
was washed in gold. He cupped a breast in his hand
and lowered his mouth to it, caressing the nipple with
his tongue, then gently with his teeth, and she whispered, "Oh God, yes," and drew her nails lightly down
his back as his mouth moved lower. The muscles in
her stomach rippled. Her thighs opened slightly. Her
hands tightened against his head as he caressed the
inside of her thigh, as his fingers slid into the wetness
there.

She gasped. She arched her hips. She said his

name. He touched her with his mouth, and suddenly she cried out and pulled him up over her, and guided him inside her.

They made love for a long time, savoring each other, playing each other, reaching a fever pitch then backing down just as they approached the edge. It was as if their bodies were tuned to the same frequency, as if their chemistry had been matched genetically. Even the best times of his marriage had never been like this.

Afterward, they lay in each other's arms, talking quietly of nothing and everything, and then they made love again. Cleary didn't remember falling asleep, but he awakened during the night, in that most silent of hours that hovered between dark and dawn. He had been dreaming that he was running on all fours and feral, fanged creatures were stalking him. Didn't take a Freud to figure out what that one meant, but still, it haunted him. He thought he was with Lana in the dream, but then she was gone, and in her place was one of the creatures.

He sat up carefully, so he wouldn't wake her, and swung his legs over the side of the bed. An opaline wash of moonlight filtered through the room, and the soft pulse of the Pacific seemed almost loud in the stillness. He glanced back at Lana, sleeping soundly on her back, a hand curled up near her chin. The sheet had slipped off her shoulders, cutting her in half just below her breasts.

Cleary noticed a gold chain around her neck. From it dangled a gold heart. It had twisted over and, when he leaned closer, he saw something was inscribed on the back. He lifted it carefully away from her skin, trying to catch the exiguous light so he could read it. She stirred; he froze. Then she sighed as if at something she was dreaming.

He deciphered the name on the back. *Sarah*.

Who the hell was Sarah?

He brought his hand away from the heart as if it had burned him, stared at her face for a long moment, at the way the moonlight limned her jaw, then he got up slowly from the bed.

He walked over to the window, opened the curtains a little, picked up his pack of Luckys from the sill. He lit one and gazed out the window as he smoked, trying not to think about the name. But it was all he could think about. He was fixated on it. He looked back at her, sleeping deeply, innocently. He wished his own sleep could have been the same. He wished he hadn't seen the heart, that he hadn't felt compelled to read what was inscribed on the back, that...oh Christ.

Cleary rubbed his eyes, then let them wander around the room until he spotted her purse. *ID. She's got to have ID. In there. Please be Lana Williams. Please don't be Sarah*. He wouldn't look. It would be better not to know for sure. If he didn't know for sure, then things could go on from here between them.

But already he was moving across the room, drawn inexorably to her purse. It rested on a chair in the corner. With a mix of regret and resolve, Cleary thrust his hand into it. His fingers brushed the wallet. *You can still take your goddamn hand outa there, buddy boy*. After all, Sarah might've been one of her names. Even Ellen had several names. Sure, Sarah Lana Williams, or the other way around, Lana Sarah Williams. But his fingers closed over the wallet, lifted it out silently.

Cleary clenched it tightly in his hand and padded back across the room with it. He went through it until he found her driver's license. He held it up to the moonlight, his vision blurred. *Put it back back back.* But now his eyes were focusing, now he was tilting it so he could read it. Now it was too late.

The name on it was Sarah Anne Thompson.

He slipped the license in the pocket of his pants, then replaced the billfold. His hands were shaking, his breathing jagged. He stared at the woman sleeping so peacefully, a beautiful imposter who had just pushed him over the brink.

TWENTY-ONE
Morning After

The Pacific at dawn was smooth as lacquer, its berylline surface lightening with the rising sun. Cleary watched as a lone pelican swooped in low over a kelp bed, its wings barely skimming a glassy swell. Then it flew off, disappearing to the west. He wished he could do the same this morning, fly out to sea and disappear from L.A., and everything that awaited him.

He stood beside a barren stretch of coast highway. This was the way he imagined the world would look after an atomic war, if it ever happened. No traffic, no people, nothing but the hot sun burning perpetually in an unnaturally blue sky, nothing but him and the hot sun. No wonder people were digging fallout shelters like there was no tomorrow.

Ten yards away, the Caddy was parked in front of an isolated phone booth, a remnant from the thirties. It was after nine, and he had been waiting patiently for almost an hour. But hey, he had no pressing social engagements. There was no one waiting anxiously for him to appear.

Then the hypnotic silence was shattered by a sharp peal from the phone. Butting out his cigarette, Cleary stepped into the booth and picked up the receiver. He listened for several moments, slowly nodded, and hung up. He stood there a moment, the sun beating hard against the glass, heating it like a greenhouse, then he opened the door and walked back to his car. He drove by rote, his mind on automatic, back to the beachhouse.

The front door was unlocked and he entered without knocking, as though he had every right to do so. The woman he had known as Lana—*her name's Sarah and she lied*, he reminded himself—was in the sunny nook of the living room, sipping coffee, wearing a pale blue robe. She was gazing out the window, her hair tumbling free to her shoulders. Cleary repressed an urge to go over to her, quietly, to lean toward her, to run his fingers through her hair. He just stood there, motionless as a corpse, watching her. The windows were open, the air awash with the sound of the ocean at high tide. She seemed oblivious to his presence.

"Seems like half of Decker Canyon's on fire."

She turned her head slightly toward him, then looked back out the window. "I thought you'd left again without saying good-bye."

He forced a smile. "After last night? I wouldn't think of it... Sarah."

Her back stiffened noticeably at the sound of her real name. The din of the Pacific and of a gentle wind were the only sounds that penetrated the subsequent uneasy silence. Cleary pulled out her driver's license from his pocket. "Feel free to jump in any time the tune moves you, honey."

She didn't say anything. She was an artist of silence, he decided. She knew how to manipulate it, mold it, sculpt it to mean anything you wanted.

He glanced down at the license. "Amazing what you can find out from just this little card, even at this time of morning. Let's see: 'Sarah Ann Thompson, born 1929, Lacrosse, Wisconsin.' No notable assets" —he dropped the license on the floor —"other than what you slide between the sheets with at night."

He stuck his hands in his pockets, looked up, recalling the rest of the facts he had been told. "Part-time model, part-time actress, currently appearing as the merry widow of Buddy Williams in a beachhouse owned by one Eddie Rosen. Judging from your performance last night, I'd say you've got a real career ahead of you."

She turned then, burying her face in her hands as her eyes misted in tears. He felt something rip open inside his chest. "Jack, please, let me explain. I tried to tell you last night when—"

"It would've gone over, too. With the real Lana

Williams back East for the month, and me..." He
smiled painfully. "Well, let's say you had an effect on
me. You made a couple mistakes, though. Your favorite little nook here looks like a new addition to me.
Don't think there're too many memories here. But
hell, I thought it might just have been redone. I
wanted to believe it. You should've taken the necklace
off with the rest of what you were wearing, though.
That's where you went wrong."

She turned back to the window, touched the gold
heart; emotion shuddered through her. He could actually see it, a ripple that swept from her spine up her
arms, to her neck, her face. "I wanted to tell you last
night," she whispered, and then her voice broke and
she covered her face again.

It was a convincing performance and he almost
bought it. Wanted desperately to buy it. But then he
thought of Nick. Of Rosen. Ellen. Nick again. Always
it came back to Nick.

Cleary stepped closer to her, a thick, dispassionate
skin growing around his heart even as he moved.
"Tell me, what? You were going to tell me it was all a
damn lie. That it? That you're on the payroll of the
man that killed my brother, and made off with my
wife."

He grabbed her roughly by the arm, jerking her to
her feet. "You look at me when I talk to you. Do
you—"

He broke off his tirade in midsentence when he
saw the bruise that spread from the lower part of her
jaw and then up along the side of her face. She

looked like a woman who'd had the hell beaten out of her.

"I didn't know they had killed anyone." She bowed her head as she spoke and touched her hand to the bruise. "I didn't. Really. Rosen told me just to get close to you, to find out what you knew about the Buddy Williams tapes."

Cleary touched her chin, lifting it. "They did this to you. Why?"

She nodded. "They came here about an hour ago. They wanted to know where you were." She raised her eyes. Desperation manacled her features. "It wasn't all a lie, Jack, you've got to believe—"

"I don't want to hear about it."

He turned away from her, pacing the room like a man possessed, trying to fit everything into a logical framework, to make sense of what he was feeling. "Why'd you do it, Sarah? Money, what? What have they got on you?"

She turned away from him again, staring out the window, finding it easier to speak to him if she didn't have to look at him. "I was seventeen years old when I came to this town, Jack. Let's just say I made a few mistakes along the way. The kind that some people won't let you forget."

Cleary's hands found her shoulders. He turned her around, gently, and his fingers slid over the bruise, drawn to it with the same inexorable tug that a moth feels toward a flame. "You didn't tell them anything when they came here this morning. Why not?"

She shrugged. "You don't want to hear about it, remember?"

Cleary resisted the urge to put his arms around her, to hold her, to lift her up and carry her over to the bed. She was a victim as much as he was. Yet he also knew that neither of them was really a victim. They had each taken the steps that had led them to this place. But why, simply to test their endurance of spirit, their willpower?

"Call them back, Sarah. Tell them I've got the tapes. Tell them I'm meeting you in three hours. At the reservoir. Do that for me."

A look of alarm swept over her face, brighter than the light, deeper than the bruise. "Jack, they'll kill you. You've seen what they've done. They're ruthless."

Cleary walked over, picked up the phone receiver, and held it out. "Make the call."

There was, she supposed, a measure of comfort to be found at the brink of the Pacific. Or at least, there had been comfort in the past. But it wasn't there for her now.

Sarah walked along the water's edge, lost somewhere inside herself. She felt the heat on her back, the warm sand against her bare feet, was aware of the relentless pounding of the surf, but all of it seemed to be happening someplace distant from her, too far away to touch.

In the short time she and Cleary had spent together, she felt like he had helped her redefine her life. Restructure it. She had confessed to the lie, after all, rather than hiding behind it, and that was something, wasn't it? And she had stood up to the bastards who thought they could run her life. But it wasn't enough. It wasn't enough because Cleary wasn't supposed to mean anything to her, but he did. He had drawn her in like no other man she had ever known.

Maybe it was this penchant of his for self-destruction. Maybe it was that desperation in him that she had hoped to quell. Hell, maybe it was just that they were great together in the sack. She didn't know anything anymore, except that he didn't have a chance of surviving against Rosen's hoods. Yes, of that much she was certain.

Something had pushed him over the edge.

She had.

And then she had tried to pull him back, but it was too late. He had slid. He was a goner. Headed toward the end.

She had reached the beachhouse again, and when she glanced up, saw a man in a dark suit standing there, watching her. *He's back. Cleary's back.* But as she neared she realized the man wasn't Cleary.

She reached the steps to the patio, paused, gazed up at him. "Who're you?"

"I'm looking for Jack Cleary."

Big deal. So's half the L.A. police force.

She climbed the steps, and slipped on her robe. "You're looking in the wrong place. There's no one named Cleary here."

The man didn't respond, and she glanced over at him. His eyes, she thought. He had a cop's eyes, cold and dark and utterly blank. They all got that look after a while, almost like an inner wall went up inside them.

"My name's Fontana." He flashed his badge. "I know Cleary didn't kill that guy in the motel. I want to help him. Where is he?"

She looked him over, did it openly, not caring what he thought. He seemed okay for a cop, and she thought she recalled Cleary having mentioned his name, but couldn't remember in what context. Good guy or bad? Yeah, when you looked at the world, when you reduced it to essentials, everything became black or white, good or bad.

"Well, it's going to take an army to save him now. He's on his way to meet some pretty ruthless guys. I tried to talk him..." She shrugged. "It's what he wants. I can't tell you why. I don't know."

She saw the crease between his eyes deepen as he nodded. "You mean Rosen's boys?" he asked. "They're the ones he's going to meet?"

"Right."

"Where? And when?"

She told him. He glanced at his watch, nodded, and started to leave.

"Do you know Cleary well?"

"We were partners," he said, and trotted back toward his car. She watched him until he disappeared around the back of the house.

Partners, she thought, then recalled what Cleary had told her last night about his former partner. "Oh God, no. Cleary, for God's sake, don't go there," she whispered.

T W E N T Y - T W O

The Rumble

As Cleary drove up to the motor court Johnny Betts called home, he cringed. The damn place looked like a home away from home for vacationing bikers and stranded Okies, for derelicts and lost souls. The parking lot was decorated with crunched beer cans, Harleys, and assorted car parts.

Betts, sporting his customary grease-encrusted black denims, engineer boots, and a torn guinea T-shirt, was leaning into the engine compartment of his Mercury when Cleary spotted him. A twelve-transistor radio hung from a hood ornament, and he heard Johnny Cash singing, "I Walk the Line."

He rolled down the window as he pulled next to the Merc. "What you doin' Betts?"

He stood up, holding a dark-tipped spark plug in one hand, and looked at Cleary. He tossed his tension-wrench into the toolbox, dropped the old plug, and grabbed a rolled-up newspaper off the side rail of the Merc.

"Did you see this, man? You made the front page. No wonder you were so hot-to-trot yesterday."

Cleary took the paper. As he glanced at the article, his features tightened. "I'm going to need that hardware I left with you."

Betts wiped his hands with a rag, then his forehead with the back of his hand. He leaned toward Cleary. "Look," he said, his voice low, "if you're going up against Roson, you're traveling a little light."

Cleary shook his head. "Thanks, kid, but all things considered I think you might want to sit this one out. No, I don't *think* it, I know it."

"Think again, Cleary. You're going to need the help. And I'm the best choice you got."

He closed the hood of the Merc and grabbed his shirt. Despite everything, Cleary laughed. Either the kid had guts or he was nuts, and whichever it was made no difference whatsoever to Cleary. He realized he respected Betts, and knew that he was seeing in him what Nick had.

Betts opened the trunk of the Merc, pulled out the suitcase, and lugged it over to the Eldorado. He climbed into the passenger seat, and set the weapons at his feet. "Let's go." He wiped his forehead. "Ten o'clock, and it's hot enough out to kill old people."

"And it's going to get even hotter," Cleary remarked, then stepped on the gas and the Eldorado took off.

A few minutes later, they were slicing through the still, torrid air at a steady forty miles an hour. As they headed up Benedict Canyon toward Mulholland, Cleary sensed the inevitable drawing near. He stared straight ahead, steeling himself, and realized he felt nothing at all—not fear, not anticipation, nothing but a sense that he was going to seize his destiny, whatever it was, and give it his best shot.

Betts, meanwhile, fumbled with the shells as he loaded the sawed-off. Sensing his anxiety, Cleary shook two Lucky Strikes out of his pack, offering one to him. It was a small gesture, but one which, for Betts, resonated deeply. He lit them both with Cleary's gold lighter, then handed the lighter to him.

"I guess Nick gave you the lighter, eh?"

Cleary looked over at him, dropping the lighter in his pocket. He knew Nick had given it to him, could remember the precise moment when it had happened, but he recalled little else about it. "Yeah, he did. How'd you know?"

Betts combed his fingers through his hair and told him about the key he had found inside the lighter, and how it had led him to the tapes.

Cleary nodded, and wondered if Nick had told him about the key. It was possible. Nick might've told him during his last bender and he could've forgotten. He literally lost days sometimes while he was drinking, blacked out, wasted, like they'd never happened at all. Time he couldn't pull back in. Time he couldn't reclaim.

Had Nick realized the extent of the incriminating evidence on the tapes? Had he known that Rosen was linked with the city's political corruption? Maybe Nick knew, but hadn't told him, fearing he would do something stupid while he was drunk. He had done plenty of that without Nick's help. He conceded he might never find out just how much Nick had figured out before his death.

High above the Los Angeles Basin, the city stretched below like some torpid beast, stupid and slow. Ringing the reservoir was an unpaved fire road, and a lifeless landscape of sycamore, mesquite, and manzanita. Everything was so parched, Cleary thought, that a fast thought would set it ablaze. A portentous silence reigned, as if the heat had even bludgeoned the locusts into submission.

Then he spotted the cars moving through the heat. Two of them. They disappeared for a moment, first the Packard, then a Fleetwood, then reappeared around a bend. They slowed, parked in the roadside underbrush directly across from him and just before the entrance to a parking area.

The man behind the wheel of the Packard stepped out, accompanied by a man with a submachine gun. The Fleetwood disgorged two more shooters, each cradling a sawed-off shotgun. Then Dibble stepped out of the back of the Fleetwood.

Five of them, Cleary thought.

The driver of the Packard took charge. He motioned the Fleetwood boys with the sawed-offs to cover the curve. "We don't want no way out for him."

"Battista," Dibble said, "we should get up above the road. We'll have a better advantage."

"Don't worry about it. Everything's under control." He gestured to the submachine gunner. "Get up on the rocks. He should be here any minute."

Cleary, crouched behind a roadside boulder, suddenly stood up. "You got that right."

Battista and his lackeys looked up and saw Cleary covering all of them with a military-issued submachine gun. "Okay, drop 'em. Right now. Everything's under control," Cleary yelled.

Battista glanced sharply at Dibble and the others. None dropped a weapon. Dibble smiled. "Hey, Cleary, you're a little outnumbered, wouldn't you say?"

"Yeah. But we got loads of enthusiasm," Betts shouted from his position across the road. He lowered his sawed-off, grinned menacingly. "Who wants to dance, *muchachos*?"

No one moved, and a deadly silence ensued. The cornered men traded uneasy glances. Suddenly Battista hissed something to Dibble and both men dove to the cover of the Packard. The others opened fire.

Cleary responded with a short, economic burst of fire. One guy fell. The second shooter dropped to one knee, pumping off a round at Betts, who flattened against a roadside boulder, then wheeled about and returned one fatal round to the man, blowing him off his feet.

Cleary ducked behind the rock as submachine gun fire ricocheted inches from his head. Betts returned the fire, knocking the submachine gunner clear off the road and into the reservoir with a twelve-gauge blast.

Betts immediately broke down his sawed-off to reload just as Battista reappeared from behind the Packard, leveling a .38 flush at him. Battista's finger was tightening on the trigger when Cleary blew him away: cold, clean, and with a vengeance.

Cleary wheeled around, hoping to knock off Dibble. Instead he found himself staring at the barrel of a .45. "Drop it, Cleary. You, too, kid," Dibble yelled from behind the Fleetwood.

They both hesitated. Then, seeing no alternative, they dropped their weapons. Cleary slowly raised his hands.

"Get down here," he barked.

Cleary climbed off the rock.

"What's it like to know you're about to die, Cleary?" asked a smirking Dibble. "Tell me about it."

Cleary stared at him, refusing to give him the pleasure of seeing him beg.

"You satisfied with your life? Happy with the world now? Got everything you want?"

"I'm about halfway there."

Dibble suddenly laughed, amazed at the brass of the man, then pulled back the hammer of the .45. "That's as far as a guy like you will ever get in this town, Jack. You can count on it."

He was about to fire when a voice behind him shouted, "It's all over, Dan."

Cleary turned slightly to see Charlie Fontana

standing at the curve in the road, beside his Ford. His
.38 was aimed at Dibble's back. "We can settle things
here or down at the station."

Dibble cautiously backed off from Cleary, lowered
his weapon, and turned to Fontana. He shook his
head, let out a contemptuous laugh. "Decisions, decisions."

Then suddenly he raised his weapon, and shot
Fontana square in the chest. Fontana returned fire,
missing his target. Cleary dove for his weapon and
raised it just as Dibble spun on him and fired.

Cleary took the bullet in his left forearm, but still
managed to squeeze off a vicious burst of submachine fire that sent Dibble flailing across the road and
into the shrubbery. The only thing he left behind as
he departed the world was a shoe, abandoned in the
middle of the dusty road.

Cleary rushed up to the critically wounded Fontana. Betts was close at his heels as Cleary knelt
down. "Oh Jesus, Charlie," he whispered.

Fontana's shirt was stained with bright red blood.
It was spreading even as Cleary lifted his head. Fontana barely pried an eye open. "You thought... I was
dirty, too... didn't you, Jack?"

The words burned.

Cleary, favoring his wounded arm, ripped open
Fontana's shirt, his face paling at the sight of the
wound. He looked up at Betts, nodded to the Ford.
"Help me get him in the car. Fast."

Then, cradling Fontana in his arms, he lifted him
as gently and as best he could, and with Betts's help,

eased him into the Ford. "Cleary." Fontana coughed. His face seemed to grow even paler, as though all the blood in his body were rushing toward his chest wound, streaming out of him. "I was under...I was setting Rosen up. When you gonna start trusting people again, Jack?"

T W E N T Y - T H R E E

Farewell Party

Cleary was seated in the corridor of the emergency room of St. John's Hospital. He stared blankly ahead, his arm propped in a sling. The bullet had passed in and out of his forearm, chewing up muscle, but causing no serious damage. He had told his story twice now. He knew there would be more questions, but no one had arrested him. They knew he had dug out the rot in the department that everyone had been smelling, and exposed it to the harsh light. No one was going to jail him for that.

But one thing still kept him here.

Fontana.

He turned his attention to his right as two uniformed officers approached. He could tell from the way they were walking that they had something official to say. The hell if he was going to go back into their impromptu interrogation room and tell it all over again. He stared stonily at them as they stopped in front of him.

"Just got word on Detective Fontana," one of them began. "Doctor says he's going to make it."

Cleary hadn't realized he had been holding his breath until he expelled it. He nodded his thanks, and willed the cops to go away as he stood. But the cop who'd spoken wasn't finished.

"Got some other news for you, too. The captain wants a word with you down at the station." A hint of a smile touched his lips. "Something about your old job."

"Okay, thanks."

His old job: sure. Just what he wanted.

He was already on his way out of the emergency room, hurrying to the Eldorado. He still had some unfinished business. The day wasn't over yet, and he didn't intend to wait for the cops to puzzle through the reports and decide what to do about Rosen. By tomorrow the little creep would have a pack of lawyers at his side, and plenty of money ready to throw around in the right direction.

Cleary wasn't going to wait for that. He knew what had to be done.

He drove fast, with determination, the hot afternoon blurring around him. He left his car in the alley behind Rosen's house, approached the rear gate, and stared inside. A walkway led up to the patio and swimming pool, and that was as far as Cleary needed to look.

Rosen was hosting a modest pool party. Cleary pegged the partygoers as West Coast hustlers and call girls. A Sinatra song was playing on a poolside phonograph, and nearby a massive bodyguard sweltered in his dark suit and Florsheims as he monitored a barbecue.

Either Rosen didn't give a damn that his men had been killed—or he didn't know about it yet. Either way, it didn't make much difference to Cleary.

He backed away from the gate before he was seen, then slipped through the backyard of the place next door, relieved to find no one in sight. A step ladder had been abandoned near the hedges that ran along the wall separating the properties, and on the ground were a pair of trimmers. Cleary moved the ladder opposite the patio, then climbed up a couple of steps and listened to Rosen. The mobster's voice traveled through the heat with the clarity of a sound through water.

"Yeah, call Monty at the Trop. Tell him fourteen point five or no deal."

Cleary took two more steps on the ladder, peered over the wall. He saw Rosen gesturing toward a young woman in a bathing suit. "Get me a fresh one, will ya honey?"

Rosen was decked out in loud Bermuda shorts and an open-collar shirt. A phone pressed to his ear, he was wrapping up a poolside conversation. "Yeah,

yeah, then track down Battista. I was s'posed to hear from him two hours ago."

So he didn't know yet, Cleary thought.

Rosen hung up, and turned to one of the hustlers relaxing in a bathing suit on a nearby chaise lounge. "I told you six months ago, we shoulda got into shopping plazas."

Cleary ducked his head again, debating about how to make his entrance. If he tried entering the front, he would have to deal with a bodyguard or two before even getting close to the pool. The back way was better, but he would have to cross fifty yards of open lawn in plain sight of everyone before he got to the pool.

The other option was going over the wall right here. The problem with that was he would be slowed down by his bad arm. He would have a hard time crawling over the wall if he had his gun in his good hand.

He wasn't sure what prompted him to look back, but when he did, he saw a woman in a uniform—a maid?—standing on the porch of the neighbor's house, watching him. Their eyes, even at this distance, seemed to lock for a moment. Then she spun on her heel and rushed back inside.

Time for decisions, buddy.

Up and over. This was it.

As he looked over the wall, he saw a young woman in a bathing suit holding a pitcher of martinis. She was about to fill Rosen's glass when Cleary placed his hand on the top of the wall and slid a leg over the side. The woman looked up and saw him. The pitcher slipped from her hand, shattering against the concrete.

"For chrissake, Sherri," snapped Rosen.

A split second later, Cleary dropped to the patio, and pulled his .38. He stuck the weapon in the back of the spatula-wielding bodyguard, and shoved him toward the pool and Rosen.

A second bodyguard approaching the pool from the house saw Cleary and stopped. In the moment it took him to figure out what was going on and start to reach for his piece, Cleary fired over his head. "Hold it, right there. Toss it. In the pool."

The bodyguard complied, lobbing his weapon into the middle of the pool, as everyone stared in silence at Cleary. "Now take a swim." He stepped forward, closer to Rosen, pushing the beefy bodyguard ahead of him. "You, too." He pushed the bodyguard, and motioned to the hustlers.

The men dove in, with the exception of the bodyguard in front of Cleary, who held his ground. "Well, what's with you? Get in."

"I don't know how."

"Time to learn."

Cleary jabbed the .38 into his back and the man reconsidered, jumping fully clothed into the deep end. He sunk, rose, sunk again. "Give him a hand, dumbos," he bellowed to the hustlers and the other bodyguard.

Cleary swung his .38 toward the call girls. "Get lost, ladies. *Now.*"

They scurried in terror across the lawn.

"What ya going to do, tough guy, shoot me?" Rosen asked, and grinned.

Cleary didn't respond. He just studied the man, intrigued, and yet a little disappointed at having the object of his quest so firmly in his grasp.

"What is this, Cleary, a domestic spat? You upset that Lana was on my side? Kinda rough, I suppose, after losing your job, wife, and brother. Yeah, I know all about you. You're a drunk and a loser."

He smiled when Cleary didn't answer. "That little lady is awful sweet, isn't she? I should have figured you were with her last night. I guess, for Lana's sake, we got there a little late. She called, by the way, just a couple hours ago to tell me she was all through playing Mrs. Williams or any other roles for me. Kinda rude after all I've done for her."

"Your problems run a little deeper than that, Rosen. I think you're avoiding the obvious."

"Whatever you got on me, Cleary, it's not going to be enough. Battista and the others must be history or you wouldn't be here right now, am I right? So they're not gonna be doing any talking, and as far as those tapes go, whatta we talking about? Buying a few cops, influencing a couple of politicians, juggling some books. Hell, you'll never pin Williams on me without corroboration."

His lip curled in a contemptuous sneer. "Stand-up fifty-buck-a-week grunts like you went out of style with the Korean War, Cleary." He made a panoramic gesture to the city. "This town runs on circuits of money and power you'll never be able to shut down."

Rosen broke off as Cleary suddenly leveled the .38

in his face, and pulled back the hammer. Rosen went pale. Then, still holding his glass, he spread out his hands and forced a smile. "You're not gonna shoot me, Cleary." He smiled. "You're not made that way."

Rosen's confidence died as Cleary pulled the trigger, and the glass exploded in his hand. Glass tinkled against the concrete. Rosen's pallor had turned ashen. Cleary lowered the .38 point-blank to his forehead. "How am I *not* made, Rosen? C'mon, tell me. I'd like to hear that again."

"You're—you're not that crazy, man."

Cleary's eyes were locked on his kill. He slowly pulled back the hammer.

"Don't do it!"

A woman's voice struck the side of his head, a voice like Lana's. Or like Sarah's—the two names were still inextricably linked in his mind. When he glanced in the direction of the voice, he saw it was the woman who had dropped the pitcher. She stood with her back to the house, clutching a gun in both hands. It was trained on him. "Don't!" she said again.

Rosen smiled, turned a hand palm up. "Good work, Sherri. Just lay it right here, Cleary."

"What good is it going to do to kill me, Sherri?" Cleary said, trying to talk her out of it. "You and Rosen won't be in the same jail."

"Don't listen to him," Rosen barked, his words hot and angry.

"Drop the gun," the woman commanded. "I swear I'll pull the trigger."

Cleary knew that if Rosen got the gun, he was dead. If he fired, he didn't doubt the woman would pull the trigger. But he would get the first round off into Rosen's brain. That's all that mattered. That was all, really, that had mattered since Nick's death.

So what're you waiting for?

Sweat poured from his forehead, his hands.

C'mon, do it. Kill the bastard.

He started to squeeze.

"Hold it," another voice shouted.

He looked up and saw a cop, his weapon ready, and backed by more blue uniforms. The scene froze. Then Cleary did it. Followed through, pulled the trigger.

The gun clicked on an empty chamber, and the sound seemed to reverberate for miles as Rosen collapsed to his knees and gasped for air.

Out of the corner of his eye, he saw Sherri drop her gun. He stared at the empty .38, wondering whether to credit the deferred execution to fate or something else. Then he turned, and walked away. He swept past the woman who had been ready to kill him without a glance, or a word.

Behind him, Rosen called, "Easy time, you crazy bastard. Two years max!"

As a phalanx of cops moved in, the lieutenant in charge stopped Cleary. "We got a call from the neighbor about a trespasser with one good wing, climbing over the fence to the Rosen residence."

He smiled. "It didn't take much to figure out who it was."

Cleary glanced back at the uniforms. "Quite a turnout for a trespasser."

T W E N T Y - F O U R

Last Boarding Call

Cleary stood on a luggage cart gazing at the faces in the midevening crowd at Union Station. He had been here ten minutes, and hadn't found her yet. He didn't even know which train she would be boarding. For that matter, he wasn't sure what he would say to her if and when he found her. He just knew that he had to see her. Once, that was all.

Over the public address system a voice announced: "Denver, Kansas City, St. Louis, Chicago, New York. Last boarding call on track number five."

Then he spotted Sarah walking under a Spanish colonial archway and passing a prewar mural. She wore a dress that moved as she moved, accentuating the soft curves of her body. Her hair was loose, silky. It shone. He remembered how it had felt against his fingers.

From a distance, her face looked devoid of expression. She clutched a carry-on bag, her only luggage. She moved with the determination of someone who had made a decision, and he suspected that hers involved leaving the past behind, abandoning it.

A porter pushing a cart stacked with luggage crossed in front of Cleary, blocking his view. When the cart had passed, he didn't see her anymore. He pushed his way through the crowd, looked up and down the gleaming stainless-steel streamliner. He considered climbing aboard, searching the cars.

No. He wouldn't do it.

He turned to leave, and there she was, standing several feet away, staring at him. Cleary took a drag from his Lucky, and watched her. Then, dropping the butt to the ground, he walked over to her.

"Hi," she said.

He nodded. In a voice that strived for a casualness that betrayed the haste he had taken to get here in time, he said, "I talked to the maid at the beachhouse. She said you were leaving town."

She smiled, but it didn't touch her eyes. The bruises had been covered with makeup, and he only noticed a trace of swelling on her jaw.

"Where you headed?"

"Out of town." Her voice was cool, emotionless.

"I came to say good-bye."

Sarah nodded. She lowered her eyes. Her lip trembled. It reminded him of how her lip had trembled that night at the beachhouse. He wondered dimly if desire and sorrow rose from the same place in the heart.

"Bye, Jack." She spoke softly, then turned and walked toward the train. She had taken several steps, when she stopped and turned back to him. "Kind of a shame when you think about it. I mean about us."

A knot of regret swelled in his chest. Regret, hunger, love, betrayal. Their eyes locked again, then she turned away and boarded the train. He stared after her a moment, then walked away and didn't look back. He was finished looking back.

The top was down on the Eldorado as Cleary and Betts headed north on Alameda, breezing through the night's heat and humidity. On the radio, the Gator was speed-rapping. "... One-oh-dos in Montrose, oh-three in Cuda-Hee and an egg-frying dog-dying one-oh-eight in South Gate on this the seventh day of a record-stompin' South Bay heat wave..."

Oblivious to the manic static on the Gator, Cleary watched a train running parallel to them on the east side of Alameda. Then he shifted his gaze back to the road.

"S'pose you'll be heading downtown Monday morning to get your badge out of storage," Betts said.

Cleary glanced out again at the train and, for a second, wondered what might have been if he had stopped Sarah from boarding the train. It was arcing east for its long night's journey. Maybe it wasn't even

Sarah's train. But if it was, which window was hers?

I'm sorry, he thought. *I'm sorry it didn't turn out like it should have.*

But on the other hand, maybe things *did* turn out as they were meant to.

"Too much has changed, Johnny. I don't know if I can play by their rules anymore." He tapped a finger against the steering wheel. "I was thinking about picking up where Nick left off."

Betts smiled to himself. It was exactly what he was hoping to hear.

On the radio, the Gator yammered on. "...so if you're looking for relief and some dancin' feet check out the cool sounds tomorrow night at the KGFJ Gator-guaranteed El Monte Stadium hop...no Levis or capris please and featuring the way-gone sounds of...the Penguins, Platters, Drifters and, for you rock cats, the stompin' sounds of Eddie Burnett and his hot new hit, let's check it out...'Sunset Strip.'"

"I know this song," Betts said as the first few bars charged out of the radio. Cleary reached for the volume knob and, to Johnny's surprise, turned it up, rather than down.

He looked over at Cleary. "Hey, I thought you were the cat who said rock and roll'd be a memory by the end of the month."

Cleary shrugged. "I can wait."

The comment was punctuated by a massive sheet of lightning strobing the entire low-ceilinged, purple-hued basin of L.A. A crashing peal of thunder followed, inspiring in Johnny a sudden laugh at the sheer joy of living.

"Well, all right." He reached up for the first few drops of rain as Cleary glanced up at the dark, impassioned sky. Then he looked over at his partner.

"We may get a little wet here, Betts."

Betts looked back at him with a look that redefined cool. "Not if you drive fast enough, Jack."

Cleary considered the aerodynamic validity of this claim, a light kindling in his eye. Then, suddenly, he punched the accelerator. The Eldorado rocketed west on Sunset Boulevard, outracing the lightning, the thunder, and the long-awaited rain.